Constantinople

BarbarianSpy

BarbarianSpy

FOR LITERARY HEAT

www.BarbarianSpy.com

"Constantinople" is a work of historical fiction. Apart from the well-known actual people, events, and locales that figure in the narrative, all names, characters, places, and incidents are the products of the author's imagination or are used fictitiously. Any resemblance to current events or locales, or to living persons, is entirely coincidental.

BarbarianSpy
Jindalee St
Toronto, NSW, Australia

Constantinople

by

Dirk Hessian

CONTENTS

Chapter One: Kazan to Novorossiysk

As soon as he had seen the truck convoy start to pull into the courtyard of the makeshift main building of the Imperial Military Academy, Pyotr dropped the weights he was working with in the exercise yard and loped down the slope and through the grove of trees that bordered one side of the river park on the rise above Kazan's river port on the Volga. As he broke through the trees, he threw himself to the ground and huddled there, arms encasing his knees, and contemplated the momentous change facing his life. He was a long way from the palaces of St. Petersburg.

He wasn't afraid; in fact the prospect of being pulled even farther away from the academy's original home in St. Petersburg, territory now firmly under the control of the Bolsheviks, excited him. Of course he would much prefer joining a regiment that would confront the Reds, but at nineteen, no one on the academy faculty was prepared to certify him as trained. Grigory Orlov, the equestrian professor, had made quite clear to Pyotr that he wasn't ready for battle.

Of course Pyotr knew that Orlov had ulterior motives for not releasing him to the battle as so many of the academy cadets had already been since they had been evacuated here from St. Petersburg—or, as the Reds now called it, Petrograd—two years earlier.

Pyotr had never attended the academy in its original imposing buildings; he had been sent to the school here in Kazan early in the previous year, 1919, by his concerned family, which had been preparing to flee into the Russian interior themselves when they sent Pyotr to Kazan. They had thought, Pyotr knew, that he would be safer here than with them. He had not heard from his father, Prince Alexi Romanov, in months and could only hope that they were faring well. None of the Russian aristocracy was faring very well at the hands of the Bolsheviks. Orlov, a classmate of Pyotr's father in an earlier Imperial Military Academy generation had been asked to take special care of Pyotr, and he most certainly had taken that charge seriously—if, perhaps, not quite in the spirit in which Pyotr's father had made the request.

What had set Pyotr's excitement and anticipation stirring was that the trucks had arrived in the courtyard to take the cadets farther to the south. This would be a new adventure for Pyotr. He had not fully enjoyed the stay in Kazan. Life had become so unsettled and confusing for him here. He had been sheltered—coddled as the youngest son in a prince's palace. He had never been expected to take on any great responsibility as was expected of his eldest brother—and also the next eldest in case the older one faltered. Pyotr would normally have been free to play his life away or to dabble in the arts, if it so pleased him. With his facility for learning languages, his mother had foreseen a career as a professor.

The Bolsheviks had changed all of that. The lives of all of the Russian nobility had been tossed up in the air. Pyotr landed in Kazan, to join the evacuated Imperial Military Academy, not because he had been destined to be a warrior but to be in what Prince Alexi Romanov had deemed would be the safest place for his young son, under the wing of Grigory Orlov and surrounded by professional soldiers.

Alexi and Grigory hadn't been close when they were in the academy together, though, and Alexi knew even less of Orlov's true nature now than he had then.

Pyotr had learned much of life—and quickly—in his year away from the opulent imperial court life of St. Petersburg and in the more Spartan environment of the exiled military academy in Kazan.

Upon seeing the trucks arrive, he needed to break away and give his future some thought. Until now he had controlled nothing. He had moved directly from a carefree life, where he was indulged in everything, to a discipline-based life, where he had been controlled, dominated, and given no choices.

He had a choice now, though. Tomorrow, the trucks would load up and leave. Departure was inevitable and could not be delayed. If Pyotr didn't show up for the mustering out, the trucks would have to leave without him. Chances were good he wouldn't even be missed in the frenetic confusion of the pack out and departure until long after the convoy had been on the road south.

He could stay in Kazan. But Kazan was nowhere, and Pyotr had no skills. How would he survive? And when the Bolsheviks showed up, what then? What good was it to be a count, the son of a prince, distant cousin to the tsar, in a world of communist revolutionaries?

"Count Pyotr, here you are. I saw you run from the exercise yard. What are you doing at the river? Did you not see the trucks arriving. We all must hurry and pack."

The large-framed Baron Vasily Bestuzhev-Ryumin, an upper-class student at the academy, a solidly built, burly young man who was truly at the academy to become one in a long line of family warriors, plopped down on the grass beside Pyotr. Like Pyotr, he'd been exercising in the yard when Pyotr had run off. Both young men were dressed just in sweat pants.

Vasily was the meatier of the two—but he was all hard muscle. He was heavily tanned, in contrast to Pyotr, because he reveled in showing his physique off and spent most of his free time in the exercise yard, working his body and competing, often roughly, for domination of the field—and he had the scars to evidence it.

He was ambitious, and rank and title conscious—and he had decided that he wanted Pyotr, who, as the son of a prince, not to mention being a beautiful young man, was a trophy worth owning. He had heard rumors that Pyotr was ripe for the plucking.

"Yes, I have seen the trucks," Pyotr answered. "I was just spending a moment alone, trying to decide whether I would leave with the trucks."

"You must, of course," Vasily said, somewhat shocked that this would even be a decision to be contemplated—and perhaps more shocked that the shy, lithe, young, still-soft third son of a prince should consider that he had a choice. "You realize that the Reds are not more than three days' march away and no one stands in their way? There will be no mercy for imperial cadets when they get here—and much less for royals such as you and me. And what would you do if you did not come with us?"

"I could perhaps learn to farm. Become someone else altogether and be productive. The Bolsheviks may be right about that—perhaps our families have not been productive enough, have not done their share in progressing society."

Vasily gave a bitter laugh. "The peasants would be nothing without us. And look at these soft hands of yours—and the silky smooth skin. You could not become a peasant before the Reds discovered you for what you are. You are not at the academy because you were cut out to be a military man—you are here to be protected by men like me."

The more powerful young man had come in close beside Pyotr and had gone from holding the younger man's hands in his to running a hand over Pyotr's chest. The hand settled on palming Pyotr's belly. Pyotr was breathing heavily, but he tried to ignore Vasily's possessive touch. He had known for some time what Vasily wanted from him. And he had contemplated whether he wanted that as well—and had yet to make up his mind. He was under no illusion that Vasily, as a senior cadet, couldn't force that issue if he wanted to, though, and Pyotr half expected, half welcomed that.

"You are talking of reasons I should try something else. I think it may be time for us to drop the titles anyway, Vasily. I think it is time to recognize that the future is not for our class anymore."

"Haven't you learned anything in the academy, Pyotr? History is with us. The Bolsheviks are rabble. We are the ones trained to fight and to rule. The peasants love us, and the Bosheviks are treating them as brutally as they do us. The serfs will rise to reinstate us. This is just a blip in history."

"And yet we are the ones who retreated here two years ago, and now are preparing to retreat even further." Pyotr had meant the statement to be ironic, but irony was wasted on one as thickheaded and medievally entrenched as the Baron Vasily Bestuzhev-Ryumin was.

"We are merely regrouping so that we can go on the counteroffensive. This is just strategic maneuvering. But enough of that. We are alone, and you know what I have intended. It could be days or weeks before we have another chance."

"Vasily, no. I came here to think. No, oh, please, no."

Pyotr's torso was encased in one of Vasily's arms, and the bigger man's other hand was stroking Pyotr's chest and belly.

"You have let me give you relief and you have given me relief, Pyotr. It was a promise that I could have you—fully."

"It was just a barracks thing. The tensions of our life here. Just something we do in the . . . Ohhh."

Vasily's mouth had gone to Pyotr's nipples and his hand had descended below the waistband of Pyotr's sweat pants and taken possession of Pyotr's cock.

"You do want me. You're hard for me," Vasily said with a low chuckle.

The two young men froze as the sound of a voice calling up from the riverfront reached their ears.

"He's calling me," Pyotr said, as he used the break in the tension of the moment to permit him to struggle out of Vasily's grasp and rise up on his knees.

"Your minder calls, yes, and you must go."

The voice was calling Pyotr's name—insistently.

"We are at the beck and call of any of the faculty, Vasily. You know that."

"Yes, but Grigory Orlov is especially attentive to you."

"My father requested that he be."

"But I'll bet your father doesn't know what Orlov has in mind for you. He wants to take you, Pyotr. Everyone knows

11

that. And everyone knows what Orlov wants from the cadets who attract him."

"Why is that different from what you want?" Pyotr had stood up and waved at Grigory Orlov, who was standing at the entrance of the academy's boathouse. Orlov spied Pyotr and beckoned to him. Vasily, who was still sitting on the ground, was outside of Orlov's range of vision.

"I am young and virile. And titled, as you are," Vasily answered, his voice edged with bitterness and scorn. "What is Orlov? He is old and is no better than one of our servants. He trained here, but he is not a general. He is only good enough to teach—and to debauch as many of the cadets as he can. He isn't worthy of you."

"He's a faculty member, and he's seen me. I must answer his call and go down to him."

"Of course you must. But beware of him. He wants only one thing from you. And you are too good to be deflowered by the likes of him."

Pyotr could find no answer to that, so he turned and worked his way down the slope to the harbor walk and then to the door to the boathouse. Orlov had already entered the boathouse. He turned in the dim light of the interior, with the reflection of the waves lapping at the side of the academy yacht sending a dancing pattern on the ceiling of the chamber.

"We leave by truck in the morning," Orlov declared.

"Do you know where we go now?" Pyotr asked.

"Yes, to the Black Sea, to Novorossiysk, to join the army of Admiral Kothak. But do not tell the other cadets. Kothak intends to impress them into service. We need every solider now, no matter how young or ill trained, to enlist in keeping the Bolsheviks from taking our Black Sea ports."

"It sounds rather hopeless," Pyotr said.

"It's never hopeless. We are the ruling class. The communists cannot sustain this for very long. The people will come to the aid of Mother Russia."

"Soon, I hope."

"That is not why I sought you out," Orlov said. He had pulled Pyotr toward him, and turned the young man so that his back was pressed into the side of the yacht that was pulled into the boathouse and that was slowly bobbing in the water next to the boathouse walkway. "We will be traveling for days, and I don't know how soon we will be able to couple again. I must help supervise the pack out and you will be busy too. Lay on your back on the decking of the vessel. I want to have you again now, while I can."

Pyotr obediently laid on the deck of the boat and lifted his legs, while Orlov took hold of the waistband of the young man's sweat pants on either side and pulled them off his legs. The heel of one of Pyotr's feet pressed into the wet decking of the boathouse walkway and his other leg raised up Orlov's torso, the young Russian count moaned softly as Orlov's mouth went to the cock that was still half hard from the recent attentions of Vasily's fist.

In short order Orlov was holding both of Pyotr's legs spread and raised, as he pressed his thighs between them and expertly fucked Pyotr's channel—as he had been doing for two months.

Late in the night, exhausted from packing up his gear, Pyotr lay awake on his barracks cot, still conflicted on whether he would be there to mount the transports in the morning. There was nothing holding him to Kazan. It was a dreary backwater city. But he castigated himself—as he had done repeatedly for months—on having let Grigory Orlov make a woman out of him. The change in his life had been just too much for him, and Orlov was too dominant. And now Vasily was after him too. Vasily was stronger and younger and better built than Orlov was—but that wasn't necessarily a good thing. Pyotr was ambivalent about what his preferences were. If only he'd been raised with some purpose in life—not to just bend with the wind.

Perhaps it would be best to take his chances away from the academy—to make a total break and to strike out on his own, no matter where it would lead him.

He heard the sounds of stifled sobbing, just a few cots down from him. He lifted his head and looked down the row of beds. Most of the young men were asleep, but not all. Vasily, almost on the opposite end of the chamber was fucking one of the cadets. Pyotr couldn't tell who it was in the dimness of the

13

moonlight coming through the unglazed windows of the old barracks building. But it could be almost any of the cadets. Vasily took whomever he wanted—even though he hadn't completed his conquest of Pyotr yet. And Vasily was someone who needed release every night, sometimes twice a day. Pyotr assumed Vasily hadn't come for him only because he was tired and didn't want to bother with the struggle. Most of the cadets had come to accept his advances, some even to seek him out for his prowess and the size of him.

A blanket was stirring on one of the other cots and was raised enough to accommodate two of the cadets under it. There was the sound of sex, but the cadets had learned to ignore those sounds in the night. They almost always went to their cots exhausted, but they were particularly so tonight.

But the sound of soft sobbing was unusual for the barracks. The first rule and lesson of the barracks was to never show weakness.

The sound was coming from the cot of the recently matriculated Mikhail Shevemetev, a slight eighteen-year-old who had appeared on the academy's doorstep almost as an orphan. In contrast to most of the other cadets who could not be sure of the plight of their families trapped behind Bolshevik lines, Mikhail had seen his immediate family slaughtered to a person from a hiding place in the family mansion on the Murmansk waterfront by a crazed mob early in the revolution.

Pyotr had felt particularly concerned for Mikhail, because he was the least of what anyone would expect to be military material. He was small and willowy and almost effeminate in demeanor. He probably only had been taken in when he appeared at the academy door because the fencing professor fancied him. And when the fencing professor grew tired of him, Vasily took him over.

Not being able to close his ears to the crying, Pyotr rose quietly from his bed and went over and sat by the prone body of Mikhail on his cot.

"What is it, Mikhail? You should sleep. You have a long journey ahead of you."

"I'm scared, Count Pyotr," Mikhail whimpered between his tears. "I cannot be brave about it as the rest of you are. The

14

communists are going to push us into the Black Sea. I have seen what they can do. I don't think I can endure more."

"There, there, all will be well, little one," Pyotr whispered. "What will be will be. And I think we need not be using titles anymore. I think such distinctions are long past needing to be dropped. I think they are much to blame for the circumstances we now are in. Transport has arrived. The academy will relocate just as it has done before. You will be fine."

"I'm scared, Pyotr. Can you hold me? You are always so good to me. One of the few."

With a sigh, Pyotr stretched out behind the small Mikhail and encased him in his arms. Almost immediately, Mikhail began moving his body against Pyotr's, who couldn't help but become aroused.

"Just go to sleep, little one. You don't need to . . ."

"It is all that keeps me sane here. Am I not nice enough for you?"

"It's not that. It's . . . ahhhh."

Mikhail had reached around and taken Pyotr's cock in his hand through the fly in his sleeping shorts. There was no denying that Pyotr was aroused. Pyotr didn't stop the smaller man when he lifted a leg over Pyotr's hip and guided Pyotr's cock to his channel opening. Pyotr slow fucked him, trying to make as little sound as possible. Mikhail's sobs had turned to sighs and quiet pants.

"Tomorrow . . . tomorrow you will be there with me, won't you, Pyotr?" The voice was thick, half clouded in the onset of an exhausted sleep.

"Yes, I will be there with you, Mikhail," Pyotr murmured, the decision once again having been taken out of his hands, giving in to the manipulation of others from all sides.

* * * *

"How do you know we are looking at an 800-mile journey in these trucks?" Vasily demanded of Pyotr.

Vasily hadn't let Pyotr out of his sight since they had all been rousted from their cots in the darkest hour of the morning.

15

The barracks lieutenant had told them all to shower, and Vasily had given him lip. Daily showering was not the regimen at the academy. Pyotr had made the mistake of saying then that it would be 800 miles packed together in the trucks—two days at least, maybe three—before they would have any chance at personal hygiene again. Vasily had let that pass at the time, but now, as they were milling around the trucks and the faculty members were belatedly trying to bring some order to who would be riding in which truck, he challenged Pyotr.

"Who told you that ours was to be an 800-mile journey? Was it Orlov? Is that what he pulled you into the boathouse yesterday to tell you?"

"Yes, he wanted me to check the academy vessel to make sure we weren't leaving anything behind that we would need. And he let slip that we are headed to the Black Sea—to Novorossiysk—to come under the command of Admiral Kothak. But he then told me not to tell any of the cadets, so please don't spread that around."

This wasn't even close to what Pyotr was pulled into the boathouse to do, but it was the best lie he could think of at the moment.

"I thought so. I didn't ask earlier, because Orlov has been stuck to you like a second skin all morning, and his being called away to help set up the passenger schedule provided the first opportunity to ask."

No more stuck to me than you have been, Pyotr thought. And Mikhail Shevemetev as well. But Pyotr knew why. Each of the three was afraid that Pyotr may slip away, and each of the three wanted to control Pyotr in his own way. This left Pyotr angry and on edge—and once again disappointed in himself that he let himself be trapped and manipulated like this. His only hope was if they were all separated in the truck assignments. Pyotr still didn't know if he would try to fade away from the journey given the opportunity. But he was angry that he may not have the opportunity to consider other options.

As it turned out, he was trapped into climbing up into the back of one of the trucks. Mikhail was assigned to another truck, drawn off by the fencing instructor who apparently hadn't lost interest in Mikhail to the extent that everyone had supposed.

And Orlov, as a faculty member, had to ride in the cab of a truck. He did arrange, however, for Pyotr to be in the back of that truck. And Vasily was in Pyotr's truck as well, having been assigned elsewhere but having made his own decision not to leave Pyotr's side for an instant until they were all on board and on the move.

They were packed in close, and there was barely enough room for all of the cadets in the bed of the truck to stretch out to sleep during the day. By the first night on the road, they had all receded into a semicomatose state from the effects of the brutal bouncing of the trucks on the primitive road south and the limited rations of water and food they were given.

Pyotr was wedged into one of the corners of the truck bed, behind the cab, and Vasily had muscled his way to his side. Orlov had repeatedly looked back through the glass in the back wall of the truck cab to check on Pyotr until Vasily had leaned his back against the glass and night had fallen, making it impossible for Orlov to pick any single cadet out of the teaming mass in the still-moving truck. The convoy had stopped every couple of hours, but only long enough for the men to take pisses and dumps at the side of the road and to, most unsuccessfully, work the cramps out of their arms and legs.

All of the men complained about the bruises that were being inflicted on their torsos, but Vasily had yelled out that the Bolsheviks would give them worse than bruises if they ever caught up with them. And then the men's complaints were reduced to mumblings under their breath. None of the cadets stood up to Vasily.

While they were still within sight of the academy buildings they were abandoning, Vasily was already touching Pyotr with his hands and trying to get as close to him as possible. Pyotr fended him off as well as he could, but by the second night on the road, he was so exhausted and only half conscious, and he just lay there, listlessly, as Vasily worked his hand into Pyotr's unbuttoned fly and slowly jacked the younger cadet off. And then Pyotr managed no more than soft whimpers and panting in shallow breaths as Vasily turned him on his belly, pulled his trousers down around his knees, covered him with his body at full stretch, and slow fucked him.

17

Most of the cadets around them were too tired to notice. Those who did notice merely thought that Vasily was doing what he had done every night in the barracks to anyone he pleased to master—by the right of the strongest. Three or four moved close to watch, savoring what Vasily was doing to the young nobleman. Many of the others wanted to do the same to him— and now that he'd been taken by one of them, might also get their chance. While Vasily fucked Pyotr, others passed the compliant Mikhail around—to one, by one, satisfy their own lust.

Vasily was grinning when Pyotr opened his eyes in the sunlight of the third day, thinking that he was the first who had fully had the finely formed third son of a prince, and a groaning Pyotr said nothing to disabuse him of that thought. Vasily had taken him more than once in the night and had whispered in his ear that he would keep on doing so as long as they were on the road.

Thus, Pyotr had the first happy thought for weeks when he saw that they were entering an urban area and one of the cadets, who have come from the south, said he thought they were entering Novorossiysk.

The happy thought evaporated, however, as they approached the wharf on the Black Sea.

Chapter Two: The Docks of Novorossiysk

A cheer had gone up along the line of trucks as the convoy conveying the cadets of the Imperial Military Academy weaved down the tail end of the Caucasus Mountains spilling into the sea at the eastern edge of the Novorossiysk harbor. From the mountains, Novorossiysk looked welcoming, with its sparkling beaches and the sun glinting off the onion-shaped dome of the Russian Orthodox church dominating the town's main square.

Even the view of the teaming mass of people on the town's wharf was heartening until the trucks grew closer and it could be seen that this wasn't the expected massing of the soldiers of General Kothak's army that the cadets were to join up with, but a huge surge of refugees trying to get onto the ships in the harbor to take them on to the Crimea Peninsula, two hundred miles off in the distance to the east across the glassy-surfaced sea. The Crimea was one of the few bits of Russia that was still held by the White Army and represented freedom and security to the adherents of the tsar.

Kothak's couriers had told the academy head that the cadets were to meet up with his army at the wharfs, but it was obvious before the convoy had even entered the town that a connection was improbable amid the chaos they could see down there in the harbor. The convoy stopped in the town square, and the cadets and faculty jumped out of the trucks to stretch their legs as a party of faculty members that included Grigory Orlov went on to the harbor to try to meet up with Kothak's staff. They returned shortly with long faces, and Pyotr overheard them reporting to the academy head.

"Kothak has already shipped his forces on to the Crimea," Orlov reported. "He says that the Bolshevik forces coalescing here are too strong for the White Army to hold Novorossiysk. He advised that the cadets should board the ships down there and join the White Army forces in Sevastopol."

"Down there? Through that teeming crowd?" The cadet, Mikhail Shevemetev, standing beside Pyotr and Vasily within hearing distance of the faculty members had been the one who had blurted that out.

"We can cut our way through that mob," Vasily boasted, looking almost ecstatic at the prospect.

Orlov drifted over to them, and speaking directly to Pyotr in a low tone, said, "Keep close to me. There are two ships down there that we've arranged to board. I want you on the same ship I take, near me."

Vasily gave him a dirty look and made sure that Pyotr was at *his* side as they boarded the trucks again to descend to the harbor.

The crowd was too thick, panicked, and crazed eyed for the trucks to have any hope of managing to part a path to get to the docks without stalling out on a pile of bodies, so they stopped at the edge of the wharf square and the cadets climbed down, formed a close wedge, and plowed their way into the melee.

It wasn't just people that impeded their progress. The refugees had brought far more of their precious possessions than they would ever be permitted to carry with them onto the ships. It was clear to all that the cargo on the ships would be elbow to elbow people, not possessions, even though over the heads of the crowd, Pyotr could see an ornate grand piano that was being manhandled up a gangplank—only to teeter briefly and then to fall into the choppy waters between the side of the ship and the quay.

As the cadets' wedge parted the ways in its journey toward the two ships now at the quay—and a third standing just off the docks and using a flatboat to ferry passengers out to the ship, refugees began to attach themselves to the sides and the back of the wedge, using the cadets to draw nearer to their goal of freedom.

Women were fighting valiantly to keep their babies and young children above the thrashing legs and feet of others—not always successfully—and there was a wailing of grief and loss floating above the heads of the crowds. Pyotr watched in horror as one woman, having dropped her baby, went under the feet of the throng herself in search for it, both—possibly mercifully—to be trampled to death. He had no time to think on this, though, as another woman was pulling at a sleeve, crying out for his protection in exchange for a jeweled tiara she was holding out in her hand. A hand from the crowd, reached out and grabbed the tiara, though, and it and the woman disappeared from Pyotr's vision as Vasily and Orlov pushed him along.

Pyotr wondered why there were only three ships in the harbor. He could see the masts of several others standing off the harbor. When he pointed these out to Orlov as they shuffled along, Orlov spat in derision. "Those are the ships of the Allies—the British, French, Italians, and Americans. They are sitting out there just to observe and report. If they support the imperials at all, it is only with their lips."

"But there's one moving toward us, into the harbor now," Pyotr said. "A huge man-of-war."

"The biggest would be the *HMS Cardiff*, the British flagship," Orlov answered. "The next largest would be the Americans' *USS Galveston*. I was told of them when I was here earlier hoping to meet up with Kothak's couriers. I don't know which that one would be."

Pyotr's attention returned to the wharf. He saw, over the top of the crowd, an elaborately carved carriage making better headway than they were from another direction in the square. Here the masses of people were making a path, in awe, for the progress of the carriage in a manner that they had shown no willingness to do for the academy's trucks.

He realized he recognized the men in the box of the carriage—and that, therefore, he knew who was inside the carriage.

"It's Olga," he cried out in recognition.

"Who?" Vasily, who was in front of him in the wedge, with Orlov behind him and Mikhail off to the side somewhere.

"The Grand Duchess Olga. My father's cousin, sister to the tsar. The people love her; that's why they are making way for her carriage."

"And probably why that ship is coming into harbor," Orlov muttered. "It must be *HMS Cardiff.* King George no doubt has no intention of leaving one of his mother's great-granddaughters stranded here."

Pyotr began bouncing up and down, attempting to get his head above the crowd and waving his cadet's cap in one hand. "Cousin Olga," he was singing out. "It's me, Pyotr. Over here."

It must have dawned on Pyotr and, alarmingly, on Orlov in the same instant that the deliverance of Olga could be a better answer for Pyotr's future than casting his lot with the cadets and Orlov, because as Pyotr more frantically sought to get the attention of Olga's footmen, Orlov was fighting to pull Pyotr's arms down and propelling him forward with the wedge. Orlov's efforts, however, were also propelling the two off to the side, causing them to break away from the wedge.

As the two stumbled into the crowd around them, Pyotr saw the slight figure of a young woman, dressed somewhat more elegantly than those around her, slipping toward the ground. He pushed toward her and reached down, catching her just in time with an arm around her slender waist and pulling her back upright. He knew well that if she'd gone under the feet of the mob, she'd have been trampled into an unrecognizable pulp of blood, bones, and ripped satin within moments. She gave him a radiant smile and murmured her thanks in the impeccable language of the Russian imperial court as he pulled her up from danger.

Pyotr realized two things instantly—that she was the most beautiful woman he'd ever seen and that he was in love.

It was only an instant of contact, though. The arms of a tall, muscular man in the uniform of a Russian naval officer were lifting the young woman away from Pyotr, and with no more than a menacing look of challenged possession on his face, the officer was guiding the young woman in a close embrace away from Pyotr. In a single breath's time, the two were lost in the crowd.

Pyotr, and Orlov who had held onto Pyotr as possessively as the naval officer had regained control of the mysterious young beauty, found themselves lost in the crowd too. In the short time it had taken for Pyotr to save the young woman, the cadet's phalanx had moved on, leaving them stranded.

Orlov didn't falter, though. He cried out, "This way," and started shoving Pyotr toward one of the docked ships.

If anything, the crowd was more angry and aggressive the closer Pyotr and Orlov got to the two docked ships. But Orlov was strong and as cruel and brutal as anyone in the milling mass of refugees. He was brandishing a strong steel cane and was using it without mercy to clear a path. It wasn't long before they were close to the ship Orlov had been striving toward and nearly at the edge of the wharf. Pyotr could see that, off to their left, the ferry now was loading up academy cadets who had managed to wedge their way to that position.

"The cadets are there," Pyotr cried out. "Shouldn't we be—?"

"We arranged for places on two of the ships," Orlov answered, raising his voice over the din of the crowd. "There, just ahead, is the embarkation point. We will take this ship."

Pyotr turned his head to take one more look at the ferry, covered now in the gray, with red trimmings, of the uniforms of his fellow cadets. He only had time to pick out the figures of Vasily and Mikhail on board the ferry before he heard the screams and saw the overloaded flat-bottomed boat flip and a cascade of gray and red slip off into the churning water of the turgid harbor.

"Mikhail and Vasily," he cried. "The cadets are in the water. Neither can swim."

But Orlov's ears were unhearing. He had already muscled Pyotr up to the embarkation booth. He was gruffly calling out to the ship's officer there—and receiving the attention that his obvious authority merited. "I have Count Pyotr Romanov, nephew to the tsar, here," his voice rang out. "He's of the Imperial Military Academy cadet contingent booked for passage on this ship. Make way for the count."

* * * *

Pyotr almost blushed with embarrassment at the deference that the ship's officers and sailors showed him when Orlov identified him as a Romanov. It had been the same out on the wharf when, despite the melee in progress, the way had been made for the grand duchess's carriage. The carriage was piled high with suitcases and trunks, which, no doubt, would all make their way on the British man-of-war, even while the masses on the docks would be lucky to get their children on a ship, not to mention any belongings.

Secretly, he had increasingly understood the crux of the revolution against his family in the two years he'd been in exile with the Imperial Military Academy cadets. His father hadn't been like this—or so Pyotr thought. His father had always treated his servants and those in the fields on their vast estates like his family. He had been as much a father figure to his serfs as Tsar Nicholas had been to all Russians. That's what Pyotr had always believed. But there had never been any question that his father was the patriarch and that all of the servants and workers in the field were there to serve him and his family. Pyotr had come to realize that he had expected every privilege that had come his way. And that it had stunted both his intellectual and emotional growth.

He had become wiser and more aware and human in these last two years in exile and being treated like any other cadet—well, almost. He didn't want to lie to himself about his special treatment, even in Kazan—and he had decided well before he arrived at the quay that, should he survive the

24

revolution, he would change his name. He would take his mother's patronymic of Apraksin and cease to be any part of a Romanov.

Orlov was not going to let that happen on the ship, though. The teacher dominated Pyotr to the extent that it seemed he had no special reverence for the Romanovs. But Pyotr was Orlov's own ticket to safety and comfort. And thus, Pyotr realized that Orlov was going to stay attached to him as long as possible and to see that everyone who would be impressed knew that Pyotr was a Romanov.

The two were ushered immediately on board, and shortly afterward the gangplank was being raised—which was no easy task. Sensing that yet one more opportunity for fleeing Novorossiysk was evaporating, the multitudes on the docks became even more agitated and an ominous keening sound built to a crescendo. The ship's sailors had to lower their bayoneted rifles and form a line to back up toward the gangplank. The rougher men in the crowd were moving to the front and closing in on the line of sailors. Mere boys had swum out and around to the end of the dock and were climbing onto it from behind the line of sailors, and the officers standing behind the lines stumbled to the side of the dock and struck the boys back into the water with the stocks of their rifles as their heads came up over the side.

The rabble was quite evidently preparing to rush the line of sailors when the first shot was fired, which was followed immediately by a volley of rifle fire that tore into the approaching refugees and sent several of them, bleeding, to the stone surface of the wharf. This gave the line of sailors only a few seconds of respite, but it was enough for most of them to turn and follow their officers up the gangplank and pull the plank up from the dock. Not all of them made it, though. Those sailors who were an instant too slow to move were overtaken by the angry mob and torn to pieces. Captured rifles were gathered up and raised toward the ship, but the sailors at the rails of the ship were quick to take aim and cut anyone down on the dock who pointed a rifle in the direction of the ship.

As the ship pulled off from the dock, a few of the younger male refugees leaped out and caught the mooring lines that hung from the sides. Any who tried to climb to the ship's rails were struck away and into the water by the butts of the sailor's rifles. All who just hung there, in hope, eventually lost their grip and fell away into the waters of the harbor before the ship had gained the open sea.

The rest of the rabble on the docks, though, turned their fury on the one remaining ship lashed to the quay. The crew of this vessel wasn't nearly as prepared for the sudden onslaught of panicked humanity, and the ship was quickly covered by maddened refugees who swarmed over it like a million ants. Pyotr was never to learn if the ship ever was able to put to sea with a load of passengers, or whether hope was lost for all by the total loss of any organization and control. Gunfire could be heard around the periphery of the wharfs; Pyotr could only hope that order was being restored.

Pyotr stood at the rails, in both disgust and shock, watching, as one by one, the young men hanging onto the mooring ropes hanging off the sides of the ship lost their grip and slid down the slimy side of the vessel and into the sea. He watched each one, in desperation, willing the young man to show that he could turn his face back to the wharf and swim the distance with strong, assured strokes. But each one whose progress he followed quickly foundered and sank from sight.

"It's a horrible sight, isn't it?" The voice was low, soft, and melodic—a stark contrast to the scene playing out before his eyes. Pyotr turned to see that the young woman he'd saved from being trampled on the wharf was standing beside him.

"I never thought to see anything like it, no," Pyotr answered. He looked around to see if either Grigory Orlov or the ship's officer who had been guiding the young woman were nearby, but he could see neither. He imagined the officer was busy helping to move the ship out to the sea. Orlov, he knew, was off trying to wrangle some sort of accommodation for them. Most of the refugees on board had to find just enough space to stretch out on the open deck or they had to disappear down into the smelly, dank hold. Pyotr assumed the deck would be where the fittest and most clever would stake their territory. He himself was prepared to bed down anywhere, just being grateful he was aboard this ship. He had yet to be able to mourn the loss of

26

Mikhail and Vasily properly—intervening events hadn't allowed for that. But he knew that in the dark of the night visions of them floundering in the water of the harbor just as the young men who had slipped from the ropes had done would invade his mind and challenge his emotions.

"I wish to thank you for preventing me from being trampled back there," the young woman said. "I forever will be grateful."

"I am glad I was where I could be of assistance to you," Pyotr answered.

"I am Katya, from Kiev," she said. "My father is Fydor Betskoy."

"The novelist? Fydor Betskoy?"

"Yes," Katya answered. "You know of him?"

"Yes—of his novels. I am Pyotr," he continued. And then after a pause, "Pyotr Apraksin. I was a student in a school in a town outside St. Petersburg . . . where my parents taught."

"But you are dressed as a cadet. A cadet of the Imperial Military Academy. And I saw you with the group of them in the harbor."

"Yes. My parents had dreams for me. But I'm afraid that I'm not a very good cadet. I have more in common with your father, the novelist, I feel. And he is . . . ?"

"I have no idea," Katya answered in a low voice. "As far as I know I am the only Betskoy alive now."

Pyotr didn't respond for several moments, but when Katya moved a hand to lay over his at the rails, she said, "and the same is with you?"

"Yes, I'm afraid so." He looked down at her hand on his, feeling an emotion more stirring and pleasant than the fear and distress that had been consuming him to this point. "I guess we are both adrift in the world then. But so far we both live."

She was about to answer, when the voice of Grigory Orlov cut into the conversation. He appeared on the other side of Pyotr at the rail and spoke sharply to Pyotr without so much as a word or look of acknowledgment for the young woman.

"I have acquired a cabin for us. It is barely serviceable, but it must do. It will be just for a night, Count Pyotr. We will be in Sevastopol tomorrow, and I'm sure we can do much better then. Come with me. I want to show you where it is."

Pyotr reddened and felt the surprise that Katya surely was exhibiting upon hearing Orlov call him count. He couldn't look at her, though. He suddenly felt cheaper and less human as a count than he had, so briefly, as Pyotr Apraksin, from a small town outside of St. Petersburg, whose parents were simple teachers. He wondered which version of him she would take as the truth. Would she think he was pretending to be a count just to save himself and to get preferential treatment on the ship? He would be crushed if she thought that.

The cabin Orlov showed Pyotr to was tiny, able only barely to hold a bunk bed, with two bureaus across a narrow aisle from them. But it had a porthole, and Pyotr knew that, by being here, they were displacing two junior officers who would have to fight the refugees for a place to sleep.

"Shall I take the top?" he asked. They were standing pressed into the side of the bunks and barely clearing the bureau's behind them. They were close together, forced to be, by the size of the cabin, and Orlov had an arm around Pyotr's shoulders. The standing room in the cabin was practically nonexistent. Orlov reached over and pushed the door to the cabin shut.

"You will have the top later tonight. But for now the bottom will suffice for both of us." He was still holding Pyotr close to him with one arm and was unbuttoning Pyotr's gray cadet tunic with his other hand.

"Professor Orlov . . ."

"Would you start denying me now, Pyotr? My protection has not stopped in Kazan. You have gotten this far toward safety only because of me. You are totally unprepared for real life. You were useless in getting from the trucks and onto this ship." Orlov was unbuckling the belt of Pyotr's trousers and unbuttoning his fly. "Can you deny it? You need me. We are not safe yet. You are alive because of me. I own you, and I will have you when I want. True?"

"Yes, professor," Pyotr answered obediently. He was breathing hard because Orlov was stroking his cock. The younger man felt the hot breath of the older on his neck, and he turned his face to Orlov and moaned as the professor took possession of his lips.

Five minutes later Pyotr was sitting on the bottom bunk and Orlov was leaning in toward him, with his fly open and his cock stroking inside Pyotr's mouth.

Fifteen minutes later Pyotr was on the surface of the bunk on the small of his back, his fists gripping the bed above him, his heels dug in the frame of the bed overhead, and Orlov crouched over his torso and pumping his ass hard with his cock.

Four hours later, Orlov was sleeping soundly and snoring on the bottom bunk, and Pyotr remained awake on the top bunk, reviewing all of the events of the day and wondering if he was the lucky one, or if Mikhail and Vasily were the lucky ones—perhaps free now from whatever challenges and miseries lay ahead, leading perhaps to a painful death anyway. Perhaps drowning was a less horrendous way to go than whatever faced Pyotr. Perhaps he would be better off if he climbed down from this bunk, went up to the deck, and slipped over the side and into the arms of the welcoming sea.

He sat up on the edge of the bunk. His thoughts then went to the young woman he'd met today, Katya. The most beautiful woman he'd ever seen, he thought, her beauty undiminished by the horrors of the day and the danger she had experienced. In spite of all that, she had exuded confidence and hope when they had talked at the ship's rail. Pyotr couldn't see her giving up as he was contemplating doing. She was stronger than he was, he felt. And Orlov was right about him not being able to survive on his own. And thus Orlov was within his rights to dominate and take Pyotr at will—at least until Pyotr was willing and able to take responsibility for himself.

The mere presence of Katya was a reason for him to live.

Pyotr climbed down from the bunk as quietly as he could and stole out of the cabin. He didn't turn toward the stairs leading up to the deck, though; he turned in the other direction, toward the one head at the end of the passageway, to relieve himself.

On the way back, he heard the sounds of moans coming from one of the cabins along the corridor. The cabin door was open just enough for him to be able to peep inside. The ship was in darkness, but the cabin had a porthole and the moon was full. Rays from the moon filtered into a cabin that was about twice the size of the one that Pyotr and Orlov were in. Instead of a bunk bed, there was a single bed. And there were a couple of chairs and furnishings that made the cabin so much more comfortable and lived-in than the cabin Pyotr had been assigned.

A senior officer's cabin.

The presumed senior officer in question was naked and crouched over the side of his bed. Another figure was in his embrace between him and the bed and facing down. Pyotr recognized the once-elegant satin dress he'd seen Katya Betskoya wearing earlier in the day. The officer, obviously the one who had guided her to the ship, had an arm wrapped around her waist. Her dress and petticoats were bunched up at her waist in back as well, revealing smooth flanks and well-turned legs. The officer was fucking her from behind with rapid, deep thrusts in her ass.

Pyotr felt outrage and violation—even though the violation wasn't his personally—well up in his gorge, and he barely was able to check his initial reaction to rush in and pull the man off Katya. It was so much worse to his sensitivities that the man was taking her in the ass.

But he stopped himself in time. These were rough times for survival. Katya was making her own choices in order to survive—just as Pyotr had done earlier that year when Grigory Orlov had made quite clear that his protection of Pyotr was contingent on Pyotr lying under him whenever Orlov beckoned. It was a decision and accommodation that had been validated twice already since they had come aboard when Orlov had taken him in the afternoon and then again that night.

And for all Pyotr knew she had requested taking the man this way to avoid complications.

Pyotr pulled away from the spectacle and quietly returned to his cabin, determined neither to ever mention this to Katya if he was so privileged as to see her again or to hold her decision for survival against her. And when he entered the cabin, he didn't climb into the upper bunk but, rather, nudged Orlov over in the bottom bunk and stretched out beside his protector and mentor. Orlov grunted, half woke, and opened his arms for

Pyotr to slip inside. Orlov slid his hand down Pyotr's bare torso and fisted Pyotr's cock. Pyotr turned his face to Orlov and they kissed. Sometime again in the night or the early morning Orlov would want Pyotr again—and Pyotr would accommodate him. Pyotr recognized that he had to make accommodations as well if he wanted to survive; if one as lovely as Katya was willing to sacrifice her dignity, he should be able to do no less.

Like Katya, Pyotr was now determined that he would live—just as long as he could.

Orlov's need came quickly. While their lips were still locked, Orlov turned Pyotr on his side, placed a beefy, hairy leg over Pyotr's smooth thigh, and pressed an already hard cock inside Pyotr's channel.

Pyotr groaned, ending the kiss with a murmured, "Yes, please be good to me. Oh, yes, god yes. Like that." He was determined to make his professor continue to want him enough to protect him—at least for now.

"So you want me now? Full surrender to me, is it?" Orlov whispered. And then he laughed when Pyotr showed his acquiescence by moving his buttocks against Orlov's groin, taking over the rhythm of the fuck.

Chapter Three: Sevastopol

The appearance of the youngest daughter, Tello, peeking into the dining hall, had occasioned the Armenian carpet merchant's hauling of his bulk out of his chair and disappearing for the few moments it took for him to escort his three young daughters back to their beds. They had been fascinated that a Russian prince had been invited to their home and had taken every opportunity to look in on the dinner guest. Pyotr had clearly heard the eldest, Silva, not more than twelve, sigh from the shadows and whisper how handsome the prince was, along with the crinolines of the three girls rustling on the staircase and the middle daughter, Arine, and Tello giggling at their love-struck older sister's dreamy declaration.

Pyotr took advantage of the brief absence of his host to open the small parchment paper-lined purse hanging from his belt and to slip a couple of slices of the roasted meat from the tray on the table, a boiled potato, and several chunks of bread in it.

The young Russian nobleman ate at one Sevastopol merchant's table or other at least twice a week in visits arranged by Grigory Orlov, who had put the word out that one of his Imperial Military Academy cadets was a Romanov prince and was interested in settling down in Sevastopol. The eldest daughter of Gurgen Petrosian was not the youngest young woman who had not so subtly been presented to Pyotr for his possible interest. None of these prospective father-in-laws had any illusions about Romanov wealth, but a prince in the family would be a prince in the family. And Pyotr was, indeed, a very handsome young man who any middle-class merchant's daughter would melt to. The Sevastopol merchants probably would have been equally impressed even if they'd known Pyotr was only a count, the son of a prince. But it was true enough that he was a Romanov, even though Pyotr had planned to take on the name Apraksin from this point forward.

Pyotr wasn't hoarding the food for himself. It was for Grigory Orlov. And Orlov wasn't advertising Pyotr's availability to dine at the homes of eligible and near-eligible daughters to marry Pyotr into a Sevastopol family. Both Orlov and Pyotr knew that within a couple of weeks, the imperial academy cadets would be moving up to the land bridge that separated the Crimean peninsula from the Russian mainland at Perekop. Until then, the military cadets—and their faculty—were housed in an abandoned military barracks near the top of one of the city's three hills. They were fed, but no better than most of the refugees trouping into the city from the Russian mainland were being fed—which wasn't enough for Orlov. Orlov essentially was sending Pyotr out on scavenging hunts in the houses of the still-wealthy Sevastopol merchants who had not yet realized that their foothold on Russia was tenuous—just as they didn't know enough about the Russian royal family to know that even though Pyotr's father was a prince, Pyotr wasn't—and wasn't likely ever to become one.

The narrow land bridge from the mainland to the peninsula, with impassable marshes on either side, had always been easily held by a smaller force against vast armies. The land approach had never been breached as long as anyone could remember. Any threat to the Crimea had always come by sea. But the White Russian army gathered on the Crimea had little respect for whatever navy the Bolsheviks could muster and, besides, the approaches to Sevastopol's harbor were being monitored by the navies of the Allies—Britain, Italy, France, and the United States. No Red navy would try to run past that gauntlet.

Petrosian returned to the table and lowered his bulk into his chair. He had a large handkerchief out and was mopping his brow from the exertion of his fast trip up the narrow stairs of his townhouse near the harbor. He looked apologetically at Pyotr.

"I'm so sorry. It's difficult to raise three daughters alone. It's been nearly a year since my Dahlia died. I would hire a governess for them, but a suitable young woman is so hard to find these days."

"They are lovely daughters. And really well behaved." Pyotr was telling the merchant what he wanted to hear. He had what he had come for now and was looking for an opening for a diplomatic departure.

"They are lively young women, yes. But they need discipline. Especially the eldest, Silva. She needs the guiding hand of a man. She will make a man an excellent, yielding wife— and she, of course, will come with a considerable dowry and a position for her husband with me, as needed. And this is such a large house. The girls are growing. It needs the sound of young children playing again. My Dahlia would be so pleased to have babies in this house again."

"Yes, I'm sure. Well, it certainly has gotten late—"

"Do you not find my eldest, Silva, attractive, prince?"

"Yes, certainly. She's a beautiful young woman."

"You could try her, if you wish."

"Try her?"

"Yes, as I said, she really needs the guiding hand of a strong man. I know that the life in the barracks must be Spartan—and a young, strapping man like you must have needs. I would, of course, be honored to have a Romanov in the family. And I know how tenuous life is in these unfortunate, unsettled times. She is upstairs in a room of her own now."

"I don't really . . . it's been a fine evening, and your daughters are lovely . . . all three of them. But there is a curfew at the barracks, and I—"

"You like them all? Well, of course, you could only marry one, but if you are attracted to all three . . . Tello is eight already, and Armenian women blossom early."

Pyotr sat there, looking dumbfounded.

"Ah, but of course this is all too sudden to think about. Where were my manners?" Gurgen was backpedaling now and sweating like a pig. "It is a lot to think about, I know. Perhaps you can come visit us for dinner again soon. The girls could sup with us, perhaps, and you could get to know them better."

"Sup with you again soon," Pyotr repeated. These were the magic words that Orlov had bade him to focus on. "Yes, yes, of course. That would be quite pleasurable."

After that Pyotr couldn't get out of there quick enough. When he had reached the entry door in the huge foyer and was exiting onto the second floor landing, where one entered the residence, with the merchant's shop on the ground floor beneath, he looked up the stairs and caught three pairs of eyes peering down at him, accompanied by wide smiles. Yes, indeed, the three young daughters were fetching—but was it really coming to this for him?

It took him a good fifteen minutes to ascend the hill to the barracks, and he might, indeed, have been worried about not making it back before curfew, if Grigory Orlov was not the faculty member responsible for curfew.

Still, he unexpectedly was challenged at the barracks door by the senior cadet, Nikolai Saltykov, who was trying to replace the lost Vasily as the cadet dominator of Pyotr. A rough peasant who had gotten into the academy because of demonstrated military talent rather than by position, he disdained the royals and made little bones about wanting Vasily's controlling position with Pyotr because of this. Only Orlov stood in his way. The academy had primitive standards in its program to toughen its cadets. Senior cadets had privileges over the junior ones, despite their family origins, and if a senior cadet was of a mind to take and keep a junior cadet for his and the junior cadet could not reason his way out of the arrangement, he was the senior cadet's for the taking. Within a few years, Pyotr would be a senior cadet himself and could do as he pleased in that regard.

"You are late, cadet," Nikolai's booming voice announced. "That cannot go unchecked." He was a florid-faced, large boned peasant of strong build and tall stature. Pyotr was no match for him in either strength or crassness—and he well knew he wasn't. He had been barely able to sidestep the senior cadet since they had arrived in Sevastopol a bare three weeks earlier.

"I have been summoned by Professor Orlov. I must go back to his chamber immediately. You may go with me, of course, if you wish to claim an infraction."

"I know where we must go, and it isn't to Orlov's room."

Nikolai was manhandling Pyotr toward the communal head and shower room just to the right of the barracks entrance. Other than the room for Orlov at the back of the barracks and those of the other faculty members on the floor above, the barracks was one long bunk room. Most of the taking that occurred between the cadets was conducted in the head at the urinals or in the showers—and mostly at times when the room was not in general use.

Pyotr had spoken in a loud voice on purpose and Nikolai had done so as well, having no low volume on his voice. This accomplished Pyotr's intent.

Grigory Orlov called out in a commanding voice as he stomped toward them from the back of the barracks. "Is that Pyotr Romanov? I wish to see him in my chamber immediately. Let him pass, Nikolai."

Orlov glowered at Nikolai, and Nikolai avoided eye contact, although the sour expression on his face showed how close to the edge of insubordination he was willing to go. But Orlov knew as well as Nikolai did that this position with the academy was Nikolai's one chance in life and that, at the foundation, Nikolai was a born soldier. Obeying his superiors was ingrained in his soul.

He pushed Pyotr away from him with such force that Pyotr almost stumbled to his knees. But Orlov was there on the other side of him, his hand going to Pyotr's arm and holding him up.

"Come, Cadet Romanov. To my chamber. I think you have a dispatch for me."

Later, in the dark of the night, Pyotr stumbled past snoring and snorting cadets, sleeping in double bunks set as closely together as possible, to his own lower bunk. He didn't have far to creep. Orlov had seen to that—making sure that

Pyotr's bunk was close to the door to his chamber. This was for Orlov's convenience rather than Pyotr's.

Orlov had made Pyotr strip and lay on his back on the single bed in Orlov's chamber while Orlov ate the meal Pyotr had brought him.

"Ugh. The beef is overdone. Next time . . . rarer."

Pyotr had almost drifted off to sleep when Orlov was finished with his meal and was ready for a different kind of feeding. He had stripped and lowered himself to the bed straddling Pyotr's chest. Pyotr opened his mouth in resignation as Orlov fed his cock in. When he was ready, Orlov lowered himself, wove his arms under Pyotr's legs and lifted and spread them, and fucked Pyotr to a mutual ejaculation.

When Pyotr crawled into his bunk, he lay there, contemplating what he'd come to. He didn't mind being fucked by men all that much. He had always assumed he would be attracted to women—and as he thought about this, the image of Katya Betskoya, who he had not seen since that night in the officer's cabin en route from Novorossiysk to Sevastopol rose up. But he'd never had sex with a woman. He had, however, had sex with men—much of it of late—and he was certainly aroused by that. The only objection he had to that was that he was being controlled by others. He was a Romanov, son of a prince. A few years earlier he would have answered to no one but his father and his eldest brother. And neither of them was often nearby. Everyone else was at his beck and call. Now, there were so many who wanted to control him.

The merchant earlier tonight, Gurgen Petrosian, wanted to control him. But perhaps not as much as others did. Perhaps what he was offering was Pyotr's ticket out of a more dreary and controlling situation. That older daughter really was a pretty little thing, and in time, Pyotr would be head of the household and merchant house. Petrosian looked like he could keel over from living too richly at any moment.

Pyotr felt the need of the latrine. He rose from the bed and moved down on the corridor between the banks of bed as quietly as he could. He was hunched over a urinal when the strong arms enveloped his chest.

"You have made me wait too long. You need to be punished for that."

The voice was low, gruff. Nikolai Saltykov.

Pyotr knew that if he resisted the result would be the same. Nikolai would just beat him into submission. He sighed and spread his legs as he felt the cock head at his entrance. And then he cried out—knowing that it didn't matter, that the cadets were accustomed to hearing and ignoring such cries from the latrine in the middle of the night but not being able to stifle the cry—as Nikolai thrust a thicker cock than Orlov had up inside him and began to pump him hard.

* * * *

Pyotr was walking down into the city of Sevastopol from the hill, one of three the city covered, that the barracks was located on. Grigory Orlov had arranged a dinner engagement for him at the home of Prince Artomon Toubetskoy, a cousin to the father of the tsar on a different branch than Pyotr was on. Toubetskoy had moved to the Crimea from St. Petersburg many years earlier amid scandal of pedophilia and had been a recluse ever since. Pyotr knew of him in whispers and frowns within the family, but of little less. He was not someone Pyotr had heard of for years. But Prince Artomon had heard of Pyotr through Orlov's speaking around that a Romanov prince was in the city. As an actual Romanov prince in the city, Toubetskoy had expressed interest in seeing another one—one he'd never heard of as far as his memory could tell.

Toubetskoy was said to be fabulously wealthy still and to lay a lavish table. So, naturally Orlov was interested in him—and in fulfilling the prince's request to see Pyotr. "He has said that if you accommodate him, he will send you away with a basket of food," Orlov had said to Pyotr. "So, of course you will give him anything he wants."

"Yes, professor," Pyotr had dutifully answered. If rumors held, though, he didn't think he could please the prince. He was too old.

Pyotr had made a contact of his own. He had sent a message to Gurgen Petrosian that said he would be pleased to return to the merchant's house for another evening—and to dine with Petrosian and his eldest daughter.

Beyond making the contact, Pyotr still didn't know what he wished to do. The cadets would be leaving in two days' time for duty at the land bridge to the mainland and he didn't know when—or if—he'd ever get back to Sevastopol if he went with them. There were the attentions that Orlov demanded, but now there too were the rougher assaults of Nikolai Saltykov, who became crueler and more brutal with each stolen encounter. Vasily had been a gentle lover in relationship to what Nikolai demanded of him.

Pyotr had left the barracks early—without permission, although Orlov would cover for him as long as he showed up for his dinner with Toubetskoy—and returned with the promised basket of gourmet food. He'd walked down into the town, lost in thought, although his eyes moved across the city, delighting in the pink- and yellow-painted buildings down near the Grafs Yilmaz Quay that dominated the western side of the long, narrow finger of water bisecting the city. The sun came out from behind a cloud and lit up the onion steeples of the intricately designed churches dotting the old city.

Pyotr could live in a city like this, he thought—as long as it remained in the hands of the White Russians. And there was no reason why it shouldn't as naturally protected as it was from the mainland. There were signs that the Bolshevik advances across several fronts were slowing to a halt. Russia was just too big to gobble up whole.

He had felt an affinity with the city from the time his ship sailed into the inner harbor and he spied the fifty-foot-marble column topped by the two-headed eagle of the Romanovs, the symbol of the tsar, towering over the rocks guarding the inner harbor entrance. He took that as an omen that here, in this city, the White Russian presence would take hold—and would, eventually become a springboard to retaking the country.

On a narrow shopping street leading down toward the quay, Pyotr was drawn up short at seeing the officer from the ship he'd come to Sevastopol on, the officer who had brought Katya Betskoya on board. Pyotr looked around, expecting to see

Katya as well, but he didn't see a young lady with the officer. Instead, he saw a young man, or who Pyotr decided was a young man, but only because he was wearing men's clothing. The youth was slight and willowy and moved with effeminate gestures and mincing steps. The officer was being very protective of him, and was letting himself be guided from window to window as the youth exclaimed his excitement at the wares on display. They went into a confectioner's shop, and Pyotr quickly moved down the cobblestoned street and onto the quay.

This was where he found Katya. She was sitting on the wide granite staircase that descended from the open-sided Greek-temple-styled open market building crowning the upper terrace of the quay. She held a flower basket and was hawking flowers. Pyotr stood, as much in shock at seeing her thus as for any other reason, and watched her work. She was good at it. She didn't try to sell them to the woman. Rather, she gave the passing men shy smiles and talked to them in low tones. And invariably they were charmed by her beauty and her flirting ways and would buy a flower from her. Her hand lingered in that of a few of the men while receiving the bloom, and they whispered to each other. Pyotr was afraid to know what might be passing between the young beauty who had captured his heart and these few men.

He waited until there were no other possible patrons nearby and then he slowly walked down the stairs. She looked up at him with a ready smile, the same smile she was giving any man who passed her by and gave her a second glance. But as he drew nearer, he could see that her smile became broader and more genuine, and her eyes twinkled. He was elated by the thought that she remembered him.

"You have taken to selling flowers?" he asked, as he drew near and crouched down on this haunches on the stairs so that they were on the same level. He didn't want to tower over her—he felt that her proper position was in the heavens, looking down on him.

"A girl has to make a living."

"You can make a living from selling flowers?"

"You can when you do it my way. Would you like a flower for your special lady?"

41

"Yes, of course. Perhaps two, because my lady is very special indeed."

He noticed that the smile faded from her face when he said this—but only momentarily. She spent a few moments picking out what seemed to be the best of the paltry bunch of flowers remaining in her basket, and Pyotr gave her far more than they were worth, he knew, in return. Then he leaned over and pushed the stems of the flowers into her cascading brunette hair over one of her delicately formed ears. He looked into her eyes, which were glistening with tears, but she lowered them, and he felt he lost a connection with her that had been fashioned without either one of them speaking.

"Where is your naval officer?" he asked, not mentioning that he had just seen him on the street of shops. "On the sail here from Novorossiysk he seemed ever by your side."

"We have parted ways," she said simply.

"And so you are truly alone . . . to make your living selling flowers on the quay."

"Yes, I'm afraid so. As I said, one does what one needs to do to survive."

"How well I know that." Pyotr's mind went to all that he endured—how he let himself be used—to survive. While he was thinking, though, a new thought—a new possibility—entered his mind.

"If you were to be offered a more stable job—one that took you off the street and gave you a roof over your head and enough to eat—would you be interested?"

"You wish me to go with you?"

"Not exactly. Not in the way you might mean," he answered. He said this, but his heart was pounding. There was nothing he would like more than if she did just that. But that wasn't the plan he had devised. "Come with me for an hour and we shall see what is possible. I cannot promise, but it is worth a try."

"And what would you want in return if I came with you?" She said it as if she still suspected that his intent was to take her to one of the cheap sailor's hotels fronting the quay for the hour that he'd asked.

He contemplated that for a moment. "If my plan works out for you, it would cost you this basket of flowers."

She looked down at the basket and the rapidly wilting small bunch of flowers and then she laughed—a somewhat bitter laugh. "That seems cheap enough of a risk. Yes, I'll go with you."

Petrosian's eldest daughter, Silva, opened the door of the merchant's house to them. Her eyes lit up and her mouth curved into a wide smile when she saw that it was Pyotr. Her eyes narrowed, however, and the smile dimmed as she saw Katya standing in his shadow. She seemed a bit rattled and uncertain when Pyotr asked to see her father in private if he was available, but she stood aside and let the two enter the foyer.

Gurgen Petrosian met them in his study. He could hardly keep his eyes off Katya, and his face became animated and his demeanor turned unctuous when Pyotr informed him that Katya was the daughter of the novelist, Fydor Betskoy. Pyotr didn't assume that the merchant would have any recognition at the mention of novelist, but he was careful to emphasize the phrase, patronized by the tsar's court, and Petrosian responded just as he had assumed he would. At that point Pyotr thought Petrosian would agree to anything Pyotr proposed, but, even though it might not have been necessary, Pyotr carried on with the totality of the plan that had entered his head when he was talking with Katya on the quay.

"You said you could not find a suitable governess for your daughters," he said. "As the daughter of a member of court, Katya has learned all of the noble women's virtues that you could possibly wish to have taught your daughters. She is an old friend of my family's, and I regret to have found out that she is here alone, one of the thousands of refugees in the city, and without a sponsor. If you were to offer her the position of governess with a modest stipend and a room and board, she could teach and chaperon your daughters—and it would be, I think, to all of our benefit."

Katya smiled at how easily the lie of family connections rolled off Pyotr's lips, but he got the impression that she approved of his use of guile.

"All of our benefit?" Petrosian asked, although Pyotr could tell that the man was already sold on the idea.

Pyotr took a deep breath and continued. "Yes, I am so interested in seeing Miss Betskoya safe and settled that I can pledge an interest in your earlier proposal to me. I must go to the front at Perekop in two days' time. But when I return to the city from there, I would be interested in discussing arrangements to join your family more intimately."

When Pyotr left the merchant's house, Petrosian was beaming with pleasure as he introduced his daughters to a somewhat bemused but willing Katya and was arranging for a manservant to go with her to her lodging to retrieve what little she had in the way of possessions.

Pyotr descended the stairs to the merchant's residence holding Katya's basket of bedraggled flowers in his hands. It already was time for him to start out for the home of Prince Toubetskoy. A harried-looking matron pushing a perambulator buggy with a baby in it and wearily responding in a monotone to the jabbering of two other small children at her side approached him as he reached the pavement. With a flourish and a smile, he handed the basket of flowers to the flabbergasted woman and melted into the crowd on the street without a look back.

It was time for not looking back, he thought, as the not-so-pleasant possibilities of the evening ahead of him flooded into his mind.

"I knew your father very well," Prince Toubetskoy said as they sat close together at a table stretching for what seemed like miles into the shadows of a dimly lit, but heavily brocaded dining room in the prince's palace. "You look quite a bit like him, although he was much younger at the time than you are now." Their initial introductions had been a bit awkward, but it hadn't taken Toubetskoy long to connect who Pyotr was after he'd seen him or for Pyotr to express surprise and an apology that Orlov had inflated his title.

Pyotr jerked slightly and trembled at the inference in the prince's voice when he said that he'd known Pyotr's father—and especially when Toubetskoy mentioned how young Pyotr's father was when he'd known him. It didn't help that the fly to Pyotr's trousers was unbuttoned and spread and that the ancient man, hunched over in a wheelchair and fishing nuts and berries off his plate with one hand, was slowly masturbating Pyotr with the other hand.

Pyotr had already eaten a lavishly presented meal and a large basket of food was sitting on the top of the table, not far from where they were positioned, as if a symbol of obligation for Pyotr to let the prince have his way with him.

"You are such a beautiful young man. Older than your father when I knew him, but a beautiful young man anyway," the old man murmured as he hunched lower over Pyotr's lap and lost interest in the food, such as it was, that was on his plate. "You will visit me again, of course."

"We go to the front in two days," Pyotr said, "but if you wish me to, I will visit you again when we return." Orlov's instructions were firm; Pyotr could do no other than accept any return invitation the prince extended to him.

And then he groaned because the prince's face was in his lap and the old man's withered lips opened over his cock head. Pyotr moaned, recognizing that, even as old as he was, the prince was still an expert at sucking cock. Some things are never unlearned especially when, as was likely with the prince, they weren't allowed to go out of practice.

* * * *

The Imperial Military Academy cadets had been in the field, on the front line at Perekop, for three months. It was a particularly cold and blustery early November, and General Pyotr Wrangel, commander of the troops there, had just given the order that the cadets were to return to Sevastopol, because they didn't have warm enough clothing for the elements.

The Red army troops, under the command of generals Semyon Budennyi and Mikhail Frunze, had been massing on the mainland across from Perekop for two months. They now outnumbered the White Army forces under Wrangel at least ten to one by Wrangel's estimation. Although no one in the White Army forces would voice it, apparently the Red Army wasn't spread quite as thin as rumor had reported. Still, the land bridge was so narrow that the approach could be defended by even fewer troops than Wrangel had at his disposal.

November 7 marked the third anniversary of the 1917 Revolution, and Wrangel's staff had determined that the Reds would probably launch a suicide assault on that date to try to take the Crimea. In many respects the defending soldiers wished they would and would get their defeat over with.

On the night leading into the 7th, a weather phenomenon occurred that happened less frequently than every fifty years in the northern Crimea. A strong wind blew across the marsh separating the mainland from the peninsula with such force that it forced the shallow water of the salt flats eastward, exposing the mud flats that the temperatures had now frozen.

Wrangel saw what this meant before the Red Army realized it. He knew that when and if the Bolsheviks recognized they could move across the full stretch of the width of the peninsula, a line that the White Army couldn't hope to hold, with impunity they could overrun Wrangel's forces and race down the 120-mile length of the peninsula to Sevastopol within a matter of days.

Wrangel determined to start moving his forces back and preparing a holding action immediately but also to send couriers back to Sevastopol to urge the acceleration of an evacuation. The evacuation had already commenced, but few had taken it seriously yet.

"A few cadets are to speed back to Sevastopol and raise the alarm," Grigory Orlov said to the cadets surrounding him. He called out the names of those who were to go. Pyotr's name was called. Nikolai Saltykov's was not. Orlov also announced that he himself would be staying on the line.

"I don't understand," Pyotr said when he was alone with Orlov. "You've always insisted that I stay close to you."

"And now I am insisting that you leave. And I also insist that as soon as you've reported to the authorities in Sevastopol that you get on any ship that will take you away from Russia—I understand that the ships of the Allied powers are willing to help with the evacuation of the city. I advise that you get as far away from Russia as possible."

"But . . ."

"I have not forgotten my promise to your father—to protect you as well as I could. I may not have done it as your father imagined until now, but I take the pledge I made seriously. Now go. Not another word, and do not tarry. I'm afraid that every hour is precious at this point. And here is a letter from General Wrangel attesting who you are and requesting accommodation immediately upon presentation of the credentials on any vessel you try to board to evacuate. This should be enough to get you a berth."

When Pyotr reached Sevastopol, he did his duty. He delivered the documents reporting General Wrangel's fears and strongly worded suggestions on an accelerated evacuation to the authorities of the city. But then, rather than go directly to the quay as Orlov had bade him to do, he ran to Gurgen Petrosian's house. When he got there, the doors to both the shop and the house were open, and both were not only deserted but also stripped of their furnishings and wares. There was no hint of where the family had gone or if they had managed to take the furnishings and goods with them—Pyotr knew that Petrosian owned one of the small ships that had been in the harbor the previous summer—or whether the house and shop had been looted in their absence.

With a heavy heart, he turned his eyes toward the quay. He had already passed the prince's palace upon his entry into the city, and it had also appeared deserted as well.

Chapter Four: Into the Black Sea

Pyotr went directly from the Petrosian house down to the Sevastopol quay. An evacuation was under way, and, in contrast to what he had experienced in Novorossiysk, this one appeared to be orderly. Ships hadn't come in directly to the quay but were standing out in harbor and being fed by small boats and tugboats drawing up to the quay in various places along the waterfront to board refugees standing in queues supervised by soldiers.

When Pyotr approached what looked like the shortest of the queues, the officer on duty, after examining the letter from General Wrangel, said that there was no question of not letting him on an evacuation ship of his choosing—and even being given priority boarding, but he advised Pyotr that it would be best for him to come back the next morning because all of the passenger ships in the harbor were already nearly full to capacity, that they were all derelict tubs, and that better-appointed ships were expected to be there the next day.

"Where are the ships taking the refugees?" Pyotr asked.

"Most are going to Constantinople," the lieutenant answered. "Some go to Samsun, directly across the Black Sea on

Turkey's east coast. Some go through to the Mediterranean either to Smyrna on Turkey's west coast or to Athens."

"I trust the Turks are prepared for this influx? There must be tens of thousands of people who need evacuated."

"Over a hundred thousand if you count the general's troops. Between you and me, the word is that his forces will be here within a couple of days, needing to be evacuated themselves. And I hope to god the Turks are prepared for this."

"I must say that this is very organized. Not a bit like the evacuation of Novorossiysk."

"You were there for that? This has all been planned by General Wrangel's staff. The general thinks of everything. We've been putting an evacuation armada together as a contingency for some time."

Pyotr looked out beyond the harbor, where the ships, some large warships, were thick in the water.

Following where Pyotr was looking, the lieutenant said, "Those aren't all evacuation ships out there. Some of the Allied nations are helping to shield the evacuation. See that large ship out there beyond the imperial column. That would be the American cruiser, the *St. Louis*, and the smaller ship beside it is the destroyer, *John D. Edwards*, also American. They and other naval vessels are escorting the refugee ships to Constantinople and then coming right back to continue to help. Come back to me tomorrow morning soon after dawn, and I'll put you right on the best ship we have out there in the morning."

Pyotr returned to the Petrosian residence. A search of all of the rooms revealed that there were still pallets in the servants' rooms and a bit of food still in the pantry. He bedded down on one of those for night, determined to be up and back at the quay shortly after dawn. He briefly considered waiting for Wrangel's retreating forces to arrive so that he could join the academy cadets again, but he decided that Professor Orlov and possibly General Wrangel might take that as an insult after they had provided for his evacuation and told him to go as soon as he reached Sevastopol.

The sound of bombs and artillery shells at the edges of the city woke him before dawn, and he bolted out of the

Petrosian house without eating anything and ran down to the quay.

Although still not as bad as the Novorossiysk evacuation had been, there was a great difference between the evacuation of today and what he had seen the previous day. Panic and urgency had set in. There still were refugees there—a great deal more than the previous day—but now there were bedraggled soldiers as well. Wrangel's army of retreat was already entering the city and trying to get on evacuation boats as well.

Most of the orderliness of the previous day had evaporated and people were no longer standing in queues at small boat pickup stations, but, rather, were mobbing whatever boat was returning to the quay from having taken other boatloads of refugees out to the larger ships, and either trying to muscle or barter their passage.

Thinking of his fellow cadets, Pyotr didn't try to board immediately but went from one end of the quay to the other, searching out evidence of the red-trimmed gray tunics of the Imperial Military Academy, now, of course, dirty and torn from months of wear and neglect. But he saw none. And he recognized none of the young men he rushed up to and turned so that he could look them in the face. None of the soldiers claimed to know anything about the cadets let alone where they were and how they had fared in the retreat.

As he searched, he saw the fleecing of the refugees that was going on by those who controlled the small boats. Boarding no longer was guaranteed save for the soldiers who could bolster their cases by brandishing whatever weapons they still possessed. The civilians were being made to surrender treasures and goods for passage.

How, Pyotr thought, was he to gain a place in one of the small boats? He still wore his red-trimmed gray tunic and he held the letter General Wrangel had written on his behalf, but he had no weapon, and he doubted a piece of paper would mean anything to the small boat captains.

As he was pondering this, he fortuitously came upon the lieutenant he'd met the previous day, who, with a small unit of soldiers at his direction, was still valiantly trying to keep the boarding of at least a couple of the tugboats as organized as his general had planned. The lieutenant was as good as the word he had given Pyotr the previous day. Proffering his apologies for the change in the atmosphere on the docks and the evaporation of the previous day's orderliness, the lieutenant put the young Romanov directly into a departing tugboat. He also apologized about what he had said about the quality of the ships; the evacuation vessels in service today weren't in better condition and accommodations as the ones of the previous day. If anything, they were even more derelict.

When the tug Pyotr was riding in cleared the inner harbor, he looked back on the city of Sevastopol, which still looked majestic and inviting in the spring sunny morning air. The double-headed eagle of his family remained proudly standing on the column on the rocks to the harbor entrance. Pyotr wondered, with regret, what the city would look like in a week's time—and what would be on top of the column to replace the imperial eagle.

When he turned his gaze out to sea, his dismay increased ten-fold. The boat he was in seemed to be headed out to an old, rusty freighter that was listing in the water and that, even from here, Pyotr could see was packed with evacuees on the decks as thickly as had been the ship he'd come to Sevastopol from Novorossiysk in. He searched for the name of the freighter on its side and saw that it was the *Rion*. He didn't have the vaguest notion what the meaning behind that name was, but he said a little prayer that it stood for "redemption" rather than "ruin."

* * * *

Having made one crossing of the Black Sea on a packed refugee ship, Pyotr didn't make the mistake of going beneath decks at all when he boarded the *Rion*. He hadn't identified himself as a Romanov, let alone a count, from the time the lieutenant got him on board a tugboat in the Sevastopol harbor. He was merely Pyotr Apraksin now, a merit cadet at the Imperial Military Academy from a village outside St. Petersburg, where his parents were both teachers.

He stood at the rails, watching the lights twinkle on in the harbor city, as twilight fell. Artillery shells lit up the horizon beyond the old city on its three hills in an atmosphere both eerie and hollow in its suggestion of celebration. Pyotr knew that neither the sounds of keening on the crowded quay or shells bursting in the air over the outskirts of the city were cause for celebration—at least for him. He wondered if he was observing, rather, the dying of a city. And tears came to his eyes, as he realized that, for the first time in his life, he was no longer in mother Russia; that he no longer was a Romanov count either, as if that had had any real meaning for a couple of years; and that he may never see his homeland again.

Despite the cold, which was accentuated out here on the water, as darkness fell over the groaning freighter, the closeness of the bodies on the deck and the fires burning in the three oil barrels set on the center of the deck made it seem warm. Relieved by their successful flight from Sevastopol and emotionally protecting themselves from thinking of the unknown future, the refugees were in a party mood.

Remarkably, space was cleared by the center fire barrel to provide a small stage, where, in succession, singers and instrumentalists, followed by folk dancers, entered the small circle of light and entertained, permitting the refugees to concentrate on something other than their own plight. At least most of them Pyotr saw were giving into the false festive mood. He began moving around the deck, as he could, and observed that not all were engaged in tension-releasing celebration. In this journey, he passed more than one birthing of the young and dying of the old and infirm, the refugees seemingly able to concentrate on entering and leaving the earth now that the trial of getting on an evacuation ship had been accomplished. He also saw and heard people suddenly remembering who wasn't there—who had been left behind—and what possessions they had lost. He also spied the pickpockets moving among the family groups, whose attentions had been concentrated on the entertainment or the births, deaths, and lamentings for lost relatives and goods, and deftly rearranging what wealth the others had managed to hold onto to that point in the evacuation.

As he watched, Pyotr realized something else. He realized that, although the supper hour was already passed, very few of the refugees were eating or drinking anything. While it was dawning on him that most might have been shortsighted enough not to take care of this need in choosing what to take with them, he realized that, in his haste, he hadn't done this either other than a small loaf of moldy bread he had found in Petrosian's larder the night before and had taken away with him.

Reasoning that the bread wouldn't get any more edible if he tried to horde any of it, he moved to a position in the dark at the side of the back of the wheelhouse, well away from the musical focus of the refugees on deck, hunkered down at the rails, closed his eyes, and slowly ate the entire loaf. It tasted good to him, mold and all, in the realization that it would probably be the last food he'd see during this journey—unless provisions had been made to feed this mob en route from Sevastopol to Constantinople.

He wondered how long the travel time was. Surely a couple of days at least as slowly as the freighter was moving.

He'd been concentrating on savoring his meal for so long that he'd finished before he realized that he was listening to the sound of sex. Curious, he rose from his squat at the rails and moved to an open door at the back of the wheelhouse. He was looking into some sort of storage room for ropes and tackles and such that were needed on deck but that the crew wanted to keep out of the elements. His eyes became accustomed to the darker interior, and he realized that he was looking at one of the junior officers of the Greek crew of the freighter taking one of the young refugee men. The refugee was belly down on a huge coil of rope, his head pointed at the door but his face looking down at the floor. He was hanging on to other objects on the floor with his fists, trying to stay steady in place, while the burly Greek stood behind and punched hard between the butt cheeks with his cock, in a brutally rough, rhythmic pounding.

"You're a handsome one. And you seem to like what you see. I'll give you a good fucking after I've done with this lad, if you like."

Pyotr realized, in shock, that the Greek sailor was talking to him. He had lingered in the doorway, adjusting his eyes to the scene, rather than drawing away in horror as soon as he realized what was transpiring. Apparently the junior ship's officer had thought this meant Pyotr was interested in what the other young man was getting as well. And, to be honest, Pyotr could not have claimed that the man had gauged his interest incorrectly.

In embarrassment, he withdrew from the doorway, but as he moved up the rails, back toward where the refugees were entertaining themselves to forget the gravity of their plight, Pyotr heard the sailor laugh a deep-chested laugh and call out. "Later then. You look a right nice piece. When you've a notion, I'll treat you right."

Pyotr stumbled back to where the crowd on deck was thicker, to the protection of the proximity of others and from the demons that plagued him as well. He had remained watching the taking at the back of the wheelhouse, because the Greek sailor had looked arousing to him. Memories of being taken roughly both by Vasily and Nikolai streamed into Pyotr's consciousness. The sailor's tunic had been open to reveal a hairy, heavily muscled chest. His face wasn't handsome, but it was a strong-featured one, commanding in the intensity of his purpose and the cruelty of his smile as he punished the channel of the young refugee. Pyotr wondered why the refugee was allowing himself to be treated like that. And then he remembered the ship officer's mention of "treating you right." Perhaps the refugee had realized he was hungry before the ones dancing about the deck had and was doing something about that.

Beyond that Pyotr couldn't deny that he was a prisoner to be taken like that too. He shook his head as if to jettison these thoughts and walked toward the flickering light on deck, seeking the proximity of other, normal refugees, whose only worries were for their own survival and that of their loved ones—and of how they were ever going to be able to start their lives over again, if they were able to survive to reach land again.

The latter thought was not an empty one. When Pyotr woke up the next morning, it was to the sensation that the freighter wasn't moving. As he stood and fisted the sleep out his eyes, he realized that it hadn't been a sensation; it was reality. The freighter's engines had foundered in the night, and there was no wind to fill its sails, which, in any event, were too scant to pull along a vessel as overloaded as this one was.

Although he heard those around him mumbling about this new danger, they seemed more vocal about being thirsty and hungry. Pyotr was thirsty and hungry too. But the multitudes around him seemed only now to be realizing that they hadn't eaten—and worse, not had even water to drink—for half a day. Grumbling was reaching a high pitch, and, indeed, the sound of that had been what had brought Pyotr up out of his sleep.

The crowd was becoming unruly. Looking to the wheelhouse, Pyotr could see that the Greek crew members now were armed with rifles and were milling around, holding a separation between them and the swirl of the refugees. The refugees were crying out to be fed and given water to drink, but there was no response from the crew. Obviously no provisions had been made to feed the evacuees.

And the *Rion* was dead in the water.

This standoff lasted throughout the day, and the refugees' attention was only diverted from begging the crew for succor by the sight of other ships, several also carrying evacuees, steaming past them. None stopped; all hovered farther off from the *Rion* as they realized the plight of the ship.

Pyotr hunkered down next to and in the shadow of the rails and conserved his energy as the long day crept on. It grew quieter after twilight, as the refugees collapsed more than retired to exhausted whimpering, moaning—and for many, dying, and wailing over the newly discovered dead.

All during the day, Pyotr had kept track of where the junior officer of the previous night was stationing himself. As darkness fell, he saw that the Greek sailor was standing in front and to the side of the wheelhouse, at the rails, apart from the other crew members. He was smoking a cigarette when Pyotr approached him.

When the sailor saw Pyotr, the young cadet was relieved to see that he was recognized.

"Hello there, my handsome little pigeon," the Greek sailor said in an amused, deep bass, keeping his voice down so that few beyond Pyotr heard him. "Have you come for some of what I can give you?"

"Can I come near so that we can talk?" Pyotr whispered. He was looking apprehensively at the shotgun the sailor was holding in a position where it could be raised and fired in an instant.

The Greek sailor seemed taken slightly aback that Pyotr had spoken in fairly fluent Greek. He looked at him, reassessing, and realizing that Pyotr wasn't just another one of the peasant or merchant-class refugees being evacuated. "You can come as near as you want," he said. And then, as if to tease and shock Pyotr, he added, "I can come inside you if you have an interest. Is that what you want?"

"Will there be food and drink if that's what I want?" Pyotr answered, without flinching, which caused the ship's officer to smile.

"Well now, I have to share my food and drink with the rest of the crew. If I was willing to share it with you, I'd have to share your ass with any of the others interested."

Pyotr hesitated for only a moment. His lips were parched and his belly was growling and they had been marooned for only a day yet. He had struggled with whether he was ready just to give up or if he wanted to live, and, although he could come up with few reasons to live, he couldn't bring himself to want to die. Not as long as there was a hint of hope, at least.

"Can I eat and drink first?"

"You can have something to drink, but food will come after I am satisfied with you. The others can wait for you, but you can wait for food."

The Greek junior officer fucked him first in a small cabin set up to accommodate two crew members on two cots with very little space between them. Pyotr was permitted to drink his fill from a flagon of water in the crew's mess, as the Greek sailor broadcast what was on offer and crew members congregated to view him and, as interested, pay whatever agreed to to the Greek sailor.

Pyotr lay sideways on the cot in the small cabin, with a pillow under the small of his back, elevating his buttocks. The Greek officer, bare-chested, hunched between his legs, holding Pyotr's legs spread, and fucked him hard. Those who were to come and had been assigned their places in line, stood around, licking their lips, pulling on their cocks, and not so patiently waiting their turns.

"You're a luscious one," The Greek said, with an appreciative laugh. "You aren't new to this, are you? You are hungry for it."

Pyotr indeed found that he was hungry for the burly Greek's attentions. He reached up to the man's hairy chest with his hands and ran his fingers through the hair on his barrel chest. The Greek looked surprised, then smiled, then lowered his lips to Pyotr's. His mouth moved down to Pyotr's nipples, where he gnawed, as his hips pistoned hard, and Pyotr groaned and moaned at the length and thickness of him.

"I can be as good as the food and drink I'm given for it is good," Pyotr said, trying to sound saucy and fulfill the role the Greek wanted him to take.

The Greek roared with laughter, and called out to those gathered around, "We've got a genuine royal courtesan here, lads. We will have to see what fancy tricks he can do for a decent supper."

After the fifth sailor, there was a commotion at the door to the cabin, and all of the sailors except for the one then fucking Pyotr and the Greek junior officer, evaporated.

"What do we have going here?" The vessel's captain asked with a gruff voice.

"He was hungry and the men are on edge from the situation on deck," the junior officer answered, as he struggled back into his tunic. Pyotr was a bit confused that the answer was so matter of fact. The Greek junior officer didn't seem to be all that concerned. "He's a prostitute, captain—and a damned fine one. He's taken the cocking well. He came to me and offered himself—for food and drink—and agreed to fucking the others as well."

The captain looked Pyotr over closely. Pyotr said nothing to contradict the Greek sailor. For one thing, he was too exhausted at this point to say much of anything; for another he had not been fed yet and wanted to do nothing to prevent that from happening.

"Bring him up to my cabin. You promised he could eat. We'll feed him there." After saying this, the captain turned and left the cabin.

The captain's cabin was above the wheelhouse. The ship's chief officer sat and watched Pyotr feed hungrily on a hearty meal and drink the beer that was offered him. And then the captain beckoned Pyotr over to his bed. By this time, warned by the looks the captain was giving him as he watched the young Russian eat, Pyotr was able correctly to discern the nature of the captain's interest.

Both stripped by the bed, without words being exchanged, and Pyotr went down on the bed on his belly. The captain stretched on top of him, and he fed his cock inside Pyotr and showed him that ship's captains could be hungry too. Before the captain had come, Pyotr heard the door to the captain's cabin open, and another senior officer entered and disrobed slowly as he watched the captain fucking Pyotr. Pyotr watched the other officer removing his clothes. He was a florid redhead, tall and thin, but made of solid muscle, and had the longest cock Pyotr had ever seen, which now was standing at a rising angle up from the flaming red hair of his crotch.

"Costas said you had a lively one up here, Captain, and might want some company. After you're done?"

"You know what I like. And he's a prostitute. We can have him together."

Pyotr groaned as the captain rose up into a kneeling position on the bed, bringing Pyotr up with him without dislodging his thick cock from Pyotr's channel. Pyotr was being clutched to the captain's chest, with one of the captain's arms around his belly and Pyotr's thigh on top of the captain's. The redheaded ship's officer knelt on the bed between Pyotr's thighs and grabbed and raised Pyotr's ankles to his shoulders while the captain tipped Pyotr's body back, raising his pelvis.

While Pyotr panted hard, groaned, and gave little cries, the redhead worked his long cock in on top of the captain's inside Pyotr's channel. When he was deeply embedded, the captain and the redhead's faces met over Pyotr's shoulder in a passionate kiss, the two moaned in harmony with Pyotr's grunts and groans, and the redhead started to stroke his cock inside Pyotr and on top of the captain's cock.

After the captain was done, he had the other officer give Pyotr some more beer and food, told Pyotr he was the best male whore they'd had since leaving Constantinople the last time, and returned Pyotr to the crew for their enjoyment.

On the morning of the third day, the U.S. cruiser, the *St. Louis*, didn't pass the *Rion* by. It came alongside, sent a water hose across to the becalmed ship to the parched-throated cries of approval of the refugees on deck, and then took the *Rion* in tow and headed for Constantinople.

Food for the refugees had already been passed across—the *St. Louis* apparently had been apprised of the *Rion*'s plight and had come to the rescue prepared. If it had come one or two days earlier, though, there would have been many more mouths to feed than there were now. Pyotr was never more proud, either before or after, in the Russian people as he was that day. As food came on board from the *St. Louis*, he watched, tears in his eyes, as the starving Russians calmly queued up to receive it and ensured that the very young, old, and inform received their rations first. Pyotr wasn't proud of the circumstance under which he himself still lived, however. But he was now thinking in terms of a survivor, not a Romanov noble. Nobility was not that prized a possession at this time in Russian history, he thought with a great deal of bitterness.

* * * *

The captain of the *Rion*, out of pride, had refused to have his freighter towed from the Straits of Bosporus at the Black Sea end of the water passage into the Sea of Marmara in the daylight, so it was twilight before the *St. Louis*, with its derelict captive in tow, entered the straits. It would be nearly eight hours before they reached the great city straddling Europe and Asia. Pyotr was standing at the rails along with the crowd of refugees, thinned out distressingly by the deaths and burials at sea over the previous few days.

He watched the lights on the shore become more densely spaced and bright as the tandem vessels steamed through the Bosporus. The first impressive sight on the approach to the city were the lights of the Rumeli Hisarı, the fortress built in the fifteenth century to guard the approach to the city from the Bosporus and, above that, Roberts College, which was founded and run by American missionaries. The redheaded ship's officer, who had shared him with the captain, had sidled up to Pyotr and gave him a running commentary of the various palaces—the Dommabahce Palace and the Beylerbeyi Sarayi—of the minarets of large, ornate mosques floating on the skyline, the docks, and markets the ships were passing en route to where the *Rion* was to be birthed at anchor in Buyukdere Bay, along with myriad other Russian refugee vessels.

"Do you know where to go and what you will do in Constantinople?" the officer asked.

"I will seek out the Russian émigré community, I suppose," Pyotr answered. "Just follow them from the ship. I have no better plans for my future than any of the others do. Just to escape the Bolsheviks."

The officer snorted. "You won't need to go far. There are Russian princes under every rock and in every sewer. You will be hard pressed to survive."

Pyotr looked at the man beside him sharply, but there was no reason to believe in his demeanor that he knew of Pyotr's parentage. As depressing—and truthful, Pyotr was sure—as what the ships' officer was telling him was, Pyotr knew he would be better in Constantinople than in Sevastopol. He had wondered constantly over the past few days what had become of Grigory Orlov and his fellow cadets. He hoped that they were to be found in Constantinople already, having been transported on ships that had not foundered as the *Rion* had.

"You could stay on the *Rion*," the officer said in a low voice. "The crew has enjoyed you—the captain also. The captain has said it would be good for the crew to have such as you on board when we travel on to Europe when the *Rion* has been overhauled. We could take you to any of several ports as long as you permitted us to make sport with you until then. You would eat well and have a ceiling over your head at night, which is better than most of these bastards will get."

Pyotr contemplated this offer. The crew had been rough on him—but none rougher than the captain and this redheaded senior officer combined. It would be a way for him to get far, far away from the refugee encampments that already taxed the Turks to the point of groaning—or at least to get ahead of the influx of Russian émigrés into mainland Europe. But then he would be completely on his own. There was no hope he could unite again with the Imperial Military Academy cadet corps, which was the last place his family knew he could be located.

"Thank you, but no. I will take my chances in Constantinople."

"You will know where we are being refitted," the officer answered before he turned and disappeared into the gawking crowd along the rails. "You have until we are patched up and sail away again to decide. The captain has said that there would be money in it for you as well. He would much rather have the crew using you on the ship than whoring on the docks and getting sliced up in their sniffing for it there."

It wasn't much of a choice, Pyotr knew. But he had seen enough of what real life had become to know that it was more of a choice than any of the refugees huddled around him had. And he was not so full of pride any more that we would reject the choice out of hand. He had already crossed that line of prostituting himself for survival. It seemed like he'd been doing that for half of his life—just not as literally as he now was doing.

"And you, sir," he asked. "Do you care if I go or stay?"

"I . . . I would much prefer you stay, of course. As would the captain."

At least there was this, Pyotr thought. At least he still had goods to sell that some wanted to buy. That too was more than most of his fellow refugees had.

Chapter Five: Constantinople

Pyotr lay on his belly on the bed in the cheap hotel, naked, and watched the American, Kenneth O'Dell, equally naked, soaping up his jaw and carefully shaving off a day's worth of blond beard. Pyotr had met the handsome, self-confident man while serving at the refugee soup kitchen near the Sirkidji train station, near the tip of Seraglio Point in Stambul. Stambul was the old city of Constantinople on the Golden Horn, where the Bosporus entered the Sea of Marmara. The main thought in the young Russian's head at the moment was that the American looked good from the rear. He was a good decade older than Pyotr was, but he had the build of an athlete, with broad shoulders tapering down to a thin waist; no hips to speak of, but heavily muscled thighs and well-shaped buttocks flaring from there.

O'Dell had told Pyotr he worked at the American embassy in Constantinople and put in time helping with the food kitchen that Helen Bristol, wife of the chief naval officer and top American diplomat in Constantinople, had set up in the center of the area in which the Russian evacuees had their temporary camps until they—hopefully—could be pawned off on Western countries. In answer to Pyotr's question of how he had kept in such good shape, O'Dell had answered that he had played American football for the 1913 national champion Notre Dame

University team and had swum vigorous laps ever since—that he had welcomed the embassy assignment to Constantinople largely because it had enabled him to swim the width of the Bosporus Strait at increasingly wider points. The notion of swimming the Bosporus was romantic to O'Dell because he had read of Lord Byron having done so.

O'Dell had told Pyotr that he was a romantic at heart, and Pyotr thought O'Dell had fucked like one, which Pyotr found both surprising and inviting.

Pyotr had no idea what American football was, but he well appreciated the swimming comments and was impressed at the stamina it must have built up in the American. His stamina throughout the night in the hotel room had, indeed, been impressive, and Pyotr was surprised that what O'Dell had told him about the university sports team he'd been on—the championship year he had played—meant that the man must be pushing thirty. Years older than Pyotr, but the man had fucked like a much stronger, more vigorous man.

Not that a lot of the men who were fucking Pyotr weren't vigorous—the Turks he went with were particularly so—but O'Dell was also the most attentive man Pyotr had lain with. He had been hard for an hour or more at intervals throughout the night, and he prepared Pyotr and worked him such that Pyotr begged for the cock and ejaculated twice to each time O'Dell ejaculated—the first time with O'Dell patiently rubbing across Pyotr's prostate until he had come. At the same time, O'Dell had complimented Pyotr on how many ejaculations Pyotr had given him through the night. He had said that he'd be hard pressed to remain awake at the embassy today because of how many times he'd wanted Pyotr in the night—and had been willingly received by Pyotr—and had exploded with Pyotr.

Pyotr hadn't gotten to sleep much either, but any time he could spend in a hotel room, no matter how primitive, was a comfort to revel in. He was particularly grateful to O'Dell for not treating him as a prostitute even though, in their coupling, there was every reason for O'Dell to know that Pyotr now was quite experienced and harbored few inhibitions. Pyotr sucked and rode a cock like a pro.

Pyotr had been in Constantinople over three months now and was working the streets, along with far too many other of the Russian evacuees, thankfully more women than young men, and sleeping on a pallet in a refugee camp tent during the day. Most of the work he was able to do was in the late evening and early night period and was conducted on the steep-sloped Horhor street near the Hagia Sofia mosque and Topkapi Palace in the old city district of Fatih.

When he first landed in Turkey, Pyotr, along with all of the survivors of the *Rion*, was taken off the ship on the Isle of Proti, which had been set up as a gateway for the refugees. Here they were deloused; their clothes, including the gray with red trim Imperial Military Academy tunic that had given Pyotr recognition and cachet, were taken from them and burned; and they were given worn but serviceable clothes to wear. Some attempt was made to record their backgrounds at this embarkation point—with Pyotr manufacturing a background that was dull enough to satisfy them without raising their interest—and to attempt to link them up with relatives and friends outside of Turkey who would take them. The more believable they could be that they would leave Turkey quickly, the more likely they were to be permitted out of the filthy, disease-ridden encampments on the Isle of Proti and to cross the water into Constantinople proper.

There were case workers there to talk to the refugees about how they could start fitting into life in Constantinople and prepare for relocating elsewhere. The official who talked with Pyotr had been quite straightforward. He had complimented Pyotr on his looks and obvious cultural refinement, had told him flatly that his best prospects were probably as a male prostitute on the streets or as a waiter in one of the expatriate supper houses, which was much the same thing, and had quickly propositioned him. Pyotr had risen and left the conversation immediately, but the kernel of reality had been set in his head.

After three days in the Proti camps, Pyotr returned to the administrative unit, found a presentable Turkish official who wanted to fuck him, and was then quickly cleared to leave the Isle of Proti behind and disappear into the Russian camps in Stambul's Fatih District on the European bank of the Bosporus.

Pyotr had immediately fallen into the routine of earning a bit of money to supplement what he could get in the refugee camp by walking the streets of the sailor bars near the Seraglio Point docks and sucking off half-drunken sailors from a myriad of nations or letting them quick fuck him against a wall in the alleys off Horhor.

The first time he was taken to one of the cheap hotels in the district was nearly the last time he had worked the streets.

He was on the street in front of one of the bars when he heard a gruff voice call out. "Pyotr Romanov. Count Romanov, is that you?"

The two young men he was standing with to while away the intervals and to give the clients a choice turned their heads toward him in surprise upon seeing that he had reacted. They were both Russian. They knew what a Romanov was. Of course Pyotr was going by the name Apraksin now.

Pyotr checked his reaction and tried to act as if he hadn't heard. Out of the corner of his eye, though, he tried to locate the face of the man who had called out to him, half recognizing the voice. Thus, he wasn't completely surprised when he saw that it was his fellow imperial academy cadet, Nikolai Saltykov, who had worked his way into taking Vasily's place between Pyotr's thighs back during the retreat from Kazan.

Nikolai was dressed like any of the other sailors off the docks now, and he was nearly as drunk as a sailor would be at this time of night. Leave it to Nikolai, Pyotr thought, to be able to disappear back into the working population.

"I'm sorry . . . who?" Pyotr murmured as Nikolai strode up to where they stood. "I don't know . . ."

"No matter," Nikolai declared, obviously understanding from the looks the other two men were giving Pyotr that they had no idea who Pyotr really was. "Come with me." He grabbed Pyotr's wrist with a tight fist, and Pyotr followed where he was being led, saying nothing to Nikolai until they were well out of earshot of Pyotr's two acquaintances.

"How did you come to be here? Are you a sailor now? What of Grigory Orlov?"

"Shut the fuck up. Yes, I'm a sailor now. One has to live. I see how you've chosen to do it. And I don't know what the fuck happened to Orlov—and care even less."

Nikolai pushed Pyotr into the doorway of the nearest cheap by-the-hour hotel, paid for the room, and manhandled Pyotr up the stairs. Once in the room, Pyotr turned to ask Nikolai more questions, but Nikolai punched him in the stomach with one hand, while uppercutting a fist into his jaw with the other, and Pyotr fell back onto the floor. Nikolai kicked him viciously in the ribs and then pulled him up by his hair with one hand and punched him in the face with the other fist. Still holding a crumpled Pyotr with one hand in his hair, Nikolai unbuttoned his fly with the other and pushed Pyotr down on his knees on the floor.

"Suck this, your majesty," Nikolai growled. "And be good at it, or I'll beat your royal ass to a pulp."

They never made it to the narrow bed in the room. After Pyotr had sucked Nikolai's cock hard, the bigger man pushed Pyotr down on all fours, mounted him like a dog, and fucked him brutally, following Pyotr across the floor and brutally thrusting and thrusting again as Pyotr sought a safety that was unattainable. At the far end of the room, beaten and with no more struggle in him, Pyotr was flipped onto his back and just lay there panting and looking dully up at Nikolai's hatred-enveloped face, as the sailor pushed his knees under Pyotr's buttocks and the small of his back and pistoned his channel hard and deep. Nikolai left Pyotr moaning on the floor and clinching his sides with no further explanation how Nikolai had gotten from the Crimea to here.

After that, Pyotr had been wary about where he was in the bar area of the Fatih District and who was coming out of the bars and onto the street. For some reason, even while Nikolai was cruelly fucking him, Pyotr had been nostalgic for the past and wondered even more now who among his fellow cadets, the academy faculty—and his own family, for that matter—was still alive and what they were having to do to remain so.

This encounter with the American embassy man, O'Dell, was only the second time Pyotr had been in a hotel room in the Fatih District—this time a far better one, but still one frequented by prostitutes and their clients. And it was the first time he'd been kept for the night. It also was the first attentive sex he'd had since Grigory Orlov was teaching him how to make the most out of taking the cock, although, as challenging as it was, Pyotr had found the double cocking of *Rion*'s captain and the redhead with the long, long cock about as arousing as he'd ever had—in just the realization that he could take two lustful men at once.

Kenneth O'Dell's commitment to Helen Bristol's refugee soup kitchen near the Sirkidji train station was for early Sunday afternoons. Their hands had touched while O'Dell was scooping gruel into bowls the first Sunday Pyotr had seen him there, and both had looked up at each other in surprise. O'Dell had smiled and Pyotr had then smiled as well. The next Sunday, taking his time in the service, O'Dell asked Pyotr if he smoked.

"I did when I could buy cigarettes," Pyotr asked.

"I'll be finished in an hour," O'Dell had said. "If you'd like to share a cigarette with me, you might stay around. I will gladly spare you one for the company."

Pyotr stayed around. There wasn't much else he needed to do until several hours after the sun went down anyway.

One of the first things O'Dell said to him as they were standing in the shadow of the train station and looking up at the Hagia Sofia mosque was, "You aren't like the rest. You seem better educated. And you carry yourself with more pride."

"My parents were teachers," Pyotr answered. "Simple village teachers outside of St. Petersburg, but I suppose they educated me better than most. And as far as carrying myself with pride, I don't know how you would reach that conclusion. There isn't much pride for a refugee from Russia in these days."

"Are you en route to joining your family?"

"I don't know if I have any family left."

"What will you do?"

"Blow with the wind, I suppose."

Then O'Dell told Pyotr about how he was an American of Irish descent who had gone to Notre Dame University in the middle of the United States and played American football there. And how he was in the American foreign service because he wanted to see the world, and that he was a long-distance swimmer, and loved the exotic atmosphere of Constantinople that left a person free to be what they couldn't be back home in the middle of the United States.

He had looked expectantly at Pyotr, but Pyotr had given no such gushing commentary on his past nor did he pursue the nuances of what O'Dell had said to him. He just thanked O'Dell for the cigarettes and expressed appreciation that the Americans were running a soup kitchen for the refugees.

"The Bristols take marvelous boat outings up the Bosporus and out into the Sea of Marmara," O'Dell said. "He's commander of the American Black Sea Fleet too, you know—and has the greatest ship to sail on. I often get invited to go with them. Helen Bristol is always looking for handsome young men to play bridge on their outings. Do you play bridge?"

"Alas no," Pyotr answered, although he, in fact, played an expert hand of bridge. He had learned that back in his sloth years as a teenager with no purpose rambling around a St. Petersburg palace. "And that all sounds like an entirely different world."

Kenneth O'Dell followed Pyotr out of the refugee camp that night, saw him soliciting sailors on Horhor Street, and obviously understood what Pyotr did in life in Constantinople.

The next time they shared a smoke in the shadow of the soup kitchen building, O'Dell was more direct.

"You aren't like the other male prostitutes."

Pyotr looked at him in surprise. O'Dell had been so matter-of-fact in saying it. This would probably mean he would be dismissed from working with Helen Bristol's soup kitchen effort, Pyotr thought.

"You know then."

"I've seen you in the alleys of Horhor Street—with other men. Furtively against the walls. I wanted to tell you that you didn't have to do it . . . to degrade yourself that way."

"We refugees do what we must do to survive," Pyotr answered. He wasn't about to show embarrassment or to apologize. But he couldn't resist adding, "So, you see how impossible it would for me to go to Mrs. Bristol's bridge outings with you."

"I would still take you, gladly," O'Dell answered. "I didn't mean to say that you shouldn't go with men if you want. I meant that, with your good looks and regal bearing, you should not have to be having sex with sailors in alleys."

"As I said, we do what we need to do to survive," Pyotr said. And then he walked off, fully expecting to receive notice not to appear at the soup kitchen the next Sunday. But the dismissal didn't come.

The two had little to say to each other the next Sunday. But that evening, when Pyotr took to the streets, he expressed surprise when O'Dell walked up to him and asked Pyotr to go with him.

"When I said you need not do it for sailors in alleys, I was saying that I would gladly pay the price to take you some place safe and clean. I was saying that I very much want to fuck you."

At that moment, Pyotr felt that whatever relationship there had been building between the two had been tarnished, but a paying client was a paying client. O'Dell hadn't batted an eye when Pyotr told him how much he would cost—and for what.

O'Dell could tell that Pyotr was embarrassed and reticent as O'Dell was asking about the various hotels, picking out the most presentable Pyotr could be made to identify, and paying for a full night at the hotel desk, which caused the hotel clerk's eyebrow to raise as much as it did Pyotr's. Both were equally surprised when O'Dell enquired about shaving toiletries, lubricant, and a large supply of condoms and paid for them. Of those items, the shaving gear took the longest for the clerk to produce, although when O'Dell asked for skin condoms, the clerk said that they, regrettably only had the cheaper, latex, variety.

"Next time I'll bring my own," O'Dell said, and Pyotr felt a shiver travel down his spine.

O'Dell hadn't shown the slightest indecision or furtiveness. When he had told Pyotr straight out in a matter-of-fact way that he wanted to fuck him—using that word rather than a euphemism, his blunt directness had shaken Pyotr. He knew then that O'Dell, a suave diplomat, was also a man of considerable experience in these matters and that he had probably discerned in Pyotr exactly what he wanted in a sex partner the first time Pyotr had walked through the food line he was serving.

Once inside the door, O'Dell didn't make Pyotr face him for the first fucking—nor did he turn on a light. He pulled Pyotr's back into his chest, wrapped his arms around the young Russian, and used his hands not only to disrobe them both, but to work Pyotr's body into high arousal. Pyotr panted as he felt O'Dell's hard cock stroking up the small of his back. Pyotr could tell the man was large and thick. He spread his thighs and began to moan as the man's cock head started rubbing back and forth over his entrance. This already was more foreplay and preparation than Pyotr had gotten during a sexual encounter since he'd left Kazan. He groaned and buried the back of his head in the hollow of O'Dell's neck as the older man's lubricated fingers began to open his channel up.

"You frighten me," Pyotr whispered. "You are a man of such standing and responsibility—and respectability. And yet you are so expert at this. You know the difference in condoms even."

"When I take you, I would wish nothing less than not to use them . . . for us to be so closely bound that not even that came between us. Perhaps in time, but. . . . You think that men of standing and respectability don't fuck other men?" O'Dell asked. And then he laughed. "In many ways you are an innocent, Pyotr. You don't seem to realize how desirable you are. How many 'respectable men,' as you say, want to fuck you from the moment they see you. And now I have you. What shall we do with you now?"

Pyotr turned his face to O'Dell's and they kissed. "Please, now. Take me . . . fuck me," he murmured when they came out of the kiss. "I want you inside me."

"It's what I want too. But I think you need some loving attention, not just sex and your money," O'Dell whispered. "And making love to you is what I want to do."

Pyotr felt O'Dell's arm go around his stomach and his feet were being lifted off the floor. O'Dell was taller and heavier than Pyotr. The young Russian tried to find the floor with his toes, but O'Dell just gave a little laugh and kept pulling Pyotr's buttocks cheeks up into his crotch. The cock head was in position and slightly, to the rim of the head, lodged inside Pyotr's hole.

"Relax. Just let yourself go, bend toward the floor, and let me control. You will enjoy this, I think—giving yourself entirely to my control."

Pyotr did so, and he moaned as O'Dell stood on the floor, holding Pyotr's jackknifed body to his crotch, and entered him to the point where his cock head was resting against Pyotr's prostate.

"Oh . . . my . . .god," Pyotr whimpered as O'Dell started to worry the prostate with his bulb—and continued to do so as Pyotr melted to his focused attentions. After Pyotr had shot off on the floor below them, O'Dell started to fuck him in earnest without changing position—until Pyotr came a second time and O'Dell came the first time.

After a brief respite on the bed, O'Dell fucked Pyotr again, slowly and languidly and completely, this time crouched facing Pyotr and hanging over his body, with Pyotr asking that the light be put on so he could watch O'Dell's muscles ripple in the act of sex. After a brief sleep, O'Dell did it again. And then in the early morning hours, yet again. He took nearly an hour each time, forcing Pyotr to be so aroused that he was begging for the cock. Pyotr could do so on demand for a client, but this was the first time that he involuntarily did so, completely lost to what Kenneth O'Dell could give him and whimpering for it.

"You seem to enjoy the sex," O'Dell said as he was standing at the basin, shaving early in the morning. He was looking at Pyotr through the mirror over the basin to where the young, glassy-eyed Russian, lay on his back on the bed. "Or is that just a well-developed act? I haven't quite figured out why men do it for money, whether some actually enjoy it."

"With you I enjoy it."

"But you don't want to be doing what you're doing—out on the street?"

"It's a way to survive."

"But you wouldn't want to be doing it if you had other options? Letting men bed you?"

"It depends on the man. It's not so bad. I haven't had other options for so long that I haven't considered it."

O'Dell returned to concentrating on his shaving. He was working on the area around his Adam's apple. It wasn't a good time to also be carrying on a conversation. But Pyotr could see the man was thinking about something, and when he finished, he spoke again.

"I know a house, near the top of Horhor. It's a very private, rather refined place. It's called Martin's Tea Room. But it's not really a room, and they don't serve tea there. And there is no one named Martin involved, although they like to keep both their employees and clients in the Westernized, refined vein. If you go there and give them my name and tell them I recommend you—which I will do if they ask me—I think you could be off the streets and out of the refugee tents."

"Do you go there?"

"I have been known to do so. If you are there, I may do so again."

Pyotr didn't answer for a while. He just lay there and watched O'Dell finish up his shaving.

When he was done, Pyotr said, in a low voice, "Come here and let me feel how smooth you are. And are there any condoms left?"

"The skin ones are nicer. They give a more natural feel to both. Raw, natural, of course, is the nicest by far. Perhaps with someone handled as carefully as they do at Martin's . . ."

"Then next time you might bring some of the skin ones? You said something like that to the hotel clerk." Pyotr was desperately fishing for an indication that O'Dell had liked the sex enough to want to do it again.

O'Dell didn't answer that, and, as it turned out, he never visited Martin's Tea Room while Pyotr was living there. But at this point, Pyotr was in no position to ask again, because he was sitting on the side of the bed, legs spread, with O'Dell standing between them, Pyotr gripping the older man's buttocks cheeks with the palms of his hands, and sliding his mouth slowly down and up O'Dell's shaft.

Pyotr had told O'Dell that he'd enjoyed the night so much that O'Dell need not pay him, but when the American embassy officer left for work that Monday morning, Pyotr found enough money on top of the bureau that he didn't have to go out on the street for the rest of the week—indeed, not before he mounted the steps of the brick townhouse at the top of Horhor with a brass plaque beside the door identifying it as Martin's Tea Room, and pressed the buzzer.

* * * *

"We don't usually go out, but this is an important client, and he can't come to us."

"That's all right, Marcel," Pyotr answered. "I haven't been out of the house for some time. If I can find it, I'll be happy to go."

"Jamir will accompany you there and back."

Pyotr knew that Jamir wasn't going along with him just to guide him. Once set up with Martin's Tea Room, Pyotr had learned, it took dynamite for a young man to pull free of it, even for a few hours, before he no longer was desirable. Martin's provided complete assurance of cleanliness and exclusively for the use of gentlemen for its clients, and a single mishap or indiscretion could shut the operation down.

Marcel was who passed for Martin. Pyotr didn't have the vaguest idea who really owned the house, and none of the other young men who serviced the clients claimed to know either. But Marcel ran it like a velvet prison. Still, Pyotr knew that Kenneth O'Dell had done him a favor by guiding him here. The men here ate well, their time with clients was regulated—indeed the quality of their clients was regulated—they were well clothed, and they each had a private room of their own. If Pyotr had stayed out on the street, he would probably be dead or diseased or hopelessly deformed by now. So, he had every reason to be grateful to Kenneth O'Dell for his introduction. The bad that came with the good, however, was that O'Dell hadn't visited Martin's and Pyotr couldn't see him outside Martin's.

Jamir escorted Pyotr to what must once have been a palace but now was cut up into apartments. Still, the apartments were large and the building was located in a wealthy part of the city and sat high on a slope overlooking the Bosporus and had

74

delicately carved stone-latticed balconies designed to let the breeze in from off the water without permitting anyone to look in. Staring up at the wall turned toward the water before they entered, Pyotr wondered if this had once been one of the sultan's harems. The building was only in a mild stage of disintegration—as opposed to the perpetual advanced stage suffered by most of the other Constantinople palaces of past sultans.

The elderly man who answered the door of the third-floor apartment looked vaguely familiar, but Pyotr couldn't locate him in his mind until he entered a room with a long dining table and saw sitting near the far end of it, in a wheel chair, Prince Artomon Toubetskoy, the cousin of his father's who he had attended to in Sevastopol.

"Oh, it is you," the prince said, as surprised to see Pyotr as Pyotr was to see him, and almost simultaneously, both enquired of the other, "How did you manage to escape Sevastopol?"

The prince recovered first. "An old Armenian lover was kind enough to give me and my faithful retainer, Boris, passage here on his own ship. And you?"

"On the *Rion*."

"The *Rion*? I heard that was one of the worst crossings."

"I would hope there were none worse, cousin. But as you can see, I now work at Martin's Tea Room. You sent for someone. But if this is an unfortunate coincidence, I can always return and send back someone who—"

"No, no. You will do splendidly. I found you to be a sweet young man. If you were only ten years younger . . ." He sighed, no doubt at the memories of many years past. "Come sit close to me here—very close. You do look so much like your father—or what he grew to look like years after I first knew him."

After the prince had unbuttoned Pyotr's fly and readjusted the covering over his own naked lap, he expertly sucked Pyotr to an ejaculation and then leaned back—before indulging a second time—and ordered up wine and stuffed figs for them both.

"You enjoy it at Martin's, do you?" he asked Pyotr.

"It keeps me alive. I perhaps wouldn't be if Martin's hadn't taken me in."

"I am surprised that Marcel allows a Romanov count outside of the walls of his best bedchamber."

"He does not know I'm a Romanov—or a count."

"Ah, and you'd prefer he didn't? You don't want the Romanov name dragged down to this? You are ashamed of—?"

"I am ashamed of nothing, cousin. We all do what we have to do to survive, and the Bolsheviks have cut the Romanovs down to a more human size, I would think."

"You would think that, would you? I would not count the Romanovs out so quickly, I don't think. I prefer to think of these Reds as a nasty interlude—that the Russian people will come to their senses when they see how these Bolsheviks rule."

"And most likely will then find a third way, cousin, I think. There are many who think the Romanovs were not much better."

"But still, I would think a better position for you would be more in keeping with your heritage, even if you have foresworn the Romanov name. Perhaps I can help you there."

Pyotr wanted to shrink from this shriveled up old man living in the past and of no use to anyone in the present. He had a vision of the prince telling him that he could come live here and be sucked off by this dried-up prune twice a day. As good as Toubetskoy was at blow jobs, Pyotr couldn't imagine of a life such as this until the old man chose to die—which then, no doubt—would mean that Pyotr would be tossed out on his buttocks. And then he'd be in no better circumstances than he was now—just older and less desirable. He could not see letting Prince Toubetskoy use up the best years of his remaining life.

"I believe I can help you obtain a waiter's job at the Parizen. Vladmir Smirnoff is an old family friend, you know."

"A waiter's job?" Pyotr asked in disbelief. "And that is a better position than the stable at Martin's."

"Yes, much. You would be more visible there. Its clientele is even more discrete than that of Martin's, and the waiters and waitresses—nearly all Russian nobles, as you are, despite your disclaimer—are free to go with whomever is attracted to them after they have finished their daily shift. I know of several of our kind who have gone on to better places from Constantinople with the help of patrons they have served there."

"Vladimir Smirnoff? He will know who I am. I'm sure we met in St. Petersburg."

"It won't matter. He will tell no one—except perhaps to your benefit—if you do not wish him to."

* * * *

One balmy night in May of 1921, two momentous changes in Pyotr's life were set in motion within an hour of each other as he was helping to serve dinner to a full room at the Parizen. The restaurant was crowded more than usual this night because the most popular night spot for the European, Russian, and American community of diplomats, naval officers, and expatriate community, the Le Grand Circle Moscovite—known in short as the Moscovite—was closed for a private function.

The first event was the sighting of the Imperial Military Academy cadet friend of his, Mikhail Shevemetev, who Pyotr had last seen flailing around in Novorossiysk harbor when the barge taking cadets out to an evacuation ship had turned over. Pyotr had been sure that Mikhail, who couldn't swim, had drowned in that incident.

Pyotr still couldn't believe it was Mikhail sitting with a severe-looking, but handsome and imposing, Turkish army officer until Mikhail saw Pyotr as well, almost broke into tears, and rose and ran to him.

"Pyotr?"

"Yes, it is me. Mikhail?"

In parody with what Pyotr had shared in first question with his father's cousin, Prince Toubetskoy, only a couple of months earlier—a question blurted out by many a White Russian refugee upon meeting someone unexpectedly they had known before escaping to Constantinople—the two asked in harmony, "How did you escape and come to be here?"

"You first, Mikhail," Pyotr said.

"I was pulled back onto the dock at Novorossiysk half drowned and put on a ship that went to Smyrna on Turkey's western, Mediterranean Sea coast. I was taken in by that Turkish army captain at the table there—the one who obviously wants me to come right back to him; he's really so possessive. His name is Edom Yilmaz and we are in an encampment not far outside Smyrna, which, you probably don't know, the Greeks now hold. He's in Constantinople on some sort of military strategy conference—and he doesn't trust me to be away from him alone."

"He is your protector?"

"Yes. In every sense of the word. It's a good arrangement for me, Pyotr. I wasn't cut out to be a soldier myself."

"I do not sit in judgment on such things, Mikhail. Not anymore. I would have no reason to do so, considering what I have had to do to survive."

"Were you in the Crimea at the fall?"

"I left just before everything collapsed. Professor Orlov made sure I got out, although I don't think he made it. The cadets were on the line facing the mainland when the Bolsheviks managed to cross."

"God certainly wasn't with us when the wind blew the water away and the mud was frozen," Mikhail said.

"I do not think God has been with Mother Russia and the tsar for several years, Mikhail, maybe longer. I am beginning to think that all of the gossips who said that the tsarevitch's blood disease and the hold that mystic, Rasputin, was able to have over the Romanovs was a harbinger of God's wrath on Russia were right. I have changed my name to Apraksin. I am Pyotr Apraksin now, the son of simple country teachers."

"I will try to remember that Pyotr, although I don't know if we ever will meet again. Captain Yilmaz is signaling me insistently to return now—and we leave again tomorrow for western Turkey. It is such a relief to know you are alive, though. I worried about you."

"And I about you," Pyotr said. And, as Mikhail was turning to return to his Turkish caption, Pyotr reached out to hold him for one last question. "And Vasily Bestuzhev-Ryumin? He went into the water when you did."

"I'm sorry, Pyotr. I never saw him again. I have no idea whether he survived. I'm sorry. I know you and he—"

"Not really, Mikhail. No. I just wonder about all of the cadets I once knew. All of that seems like it was in some far off, separate life."

"I know what you mean. I must go, though, Pyotr. The best of luck for you for the future. I am so happy to know that you live."

"And I you as well."

As Mikhail went back to his table and to his Turkish captain, who put a possessive arm around his neck as he sat down, Pyotr's mind went back to all of those who had been in his life and had suddenly dropped out of it—his father and mother, and his siblings. And then, later, in Kazan, with the Imperial Military Academy, his fellow cadets, particularly Vasily and Mikhail, and, of course, Grigory Orlov, his professor and protector. The man who had initiated him and controlled him in such a similar, possessive way as Mikhail's Turkish captain was now controlling him. But, above all, Katya Betskoya, the Kiev beauty who had stolen his breath away in just a few moments of contact, but who was almost constantly in his thoughts now. What of her? Had she managed to escape Sevastopol? And, if so, where was she? Was she, even now, here in Constantinople, just a few blocks away from here? Would he stumble on her some day in the same manner as Mikhail had just appeared? And would there be a Turkish captain with his possessive arm around her shoulders when they did meet?

The Turkish captain and Mikhail left soon thereafter. But as they were leaving, a middle-aged Greek, obviously from his dress and demeanor very wealthy and important, came in for dinner. Pyotr was assigned to serve him, and the Greek showed interest in the young Russian man immediately—an interest that they did not need to define, as the Greek had seen Pyotr at Martin's Tea Room weeks before.

"I have seen you at Martin's," the Greek said, as Pyotr brought him his check.

"Yes, sir," Pyotr answered. There was no reason for him to lie.

"I missed you not being there. I came once explicitly to engage your services, and you weren't there."

"Sorry, sir."

"Perhaps you would be interested in going with me tonight?" He was doling out money on the tray Pyotr had provided to pay his bill—and he was doling out over twice the cost of his meal.

"If you wish, sir."

"You do not find me too old or repulsive?"

"No, sir. You look just fine to me, sir." And indeed, although old enough to be gray-haired, the Greek had kept himself in presentable shape.

The Greek, who turned out to be a merchant with interests across the Aegean region and into the Black Sea, was named Theo Maneates. He fucked Pyotr in the backseat of a big, black motorcar parked just down the street from the restaurant. Pyotr gave him exemplary servicing, and Theo Maneates was quite pleased.

"You have a fine car here," Pyotr whispered as he sat in Maneates's lap, and the Greek's cock was softening inside him.

"Would you like to drive it?"

"Drive it? I can't drive a motorcar."

"Would you like to learn?"

"Certainly. Someday. That would indeed be an adventure."

"Would you like to learn to drive someday soon—and come work for me as my chauffeur? Driving this motorcar? My chauffeur has died and I need a replacement—one who is as willing and entertaining as you. My wife does not like me to leave the house in the evening when she is in Constantinople. That's why it took me so long to come visit you at Martin's. She's very suspicious. But the chauffeur's room is just over the garage at my residence. You could drive me in my car during the day—and I would pay you well if I could drive you in the chauffeur's room at my whim and when I could manage it in the night."

"I can tell the idea is arousing to you," Pyotr said, with a low laugh. "You are rising inside me again."

"Yes, I want you again now. Are you interested in my business proposition?"

"Why not," Pyotr answered. And why not indeed, he thought. It would be a less taxing job, a full step up from waitering during the day and prostituting himself to whoever wanted him at night. The man was middle aged and a bit fat, but he was not bad looking, he fucked with vigor, he evidently had a full purse, and he had been able to go hard twice in the same evening.

Chapter Six: Smyrna

If he wasn't so frightened; hot, even at midnight; and despairing of all the misery around him, Pyotr would have had to laugh. This was the third panicked evacuation he had been beset with within the last two years. And of the three, this one provided the least assurance that he would survive. Only the strong sea breeze coming in across the docks of the western Turkish harbor city of Smyrna was keeping the fires—and the blistering heat from the fires—in the Greek and Armenian quarters of the city from reaching where he and thousands of others were huddled on the city's cobble-stoned quay, hoping for deliverance by Greek ships. They all had their faces turned to the sea to spy the promised Greek ships coming through the cordon that the Allied navies had established beyond the inner harbor to protect the evacuation ships—if they were ever to come.

It wasn't the Bolsheviks he was fleeing now. It was the Turks and not because he was Russian but because he might be mistaken for a Greek or Armenian. Much of Turkey was held as an occupied nation by the Greeks—eternally hated on religious, ethnic, and traditional territorial grounds—at this time because the Greeks had been on the winning side of World War I and the Turks had not. Much of the Turkish animosity toward the Armenians in their midst—beyond the fact that Armenians were

Christian—stemmed, much as the origin of hatred of Jews elsewhere in the world, from the Armenian community's virtual family-based tight-fisted control of the economy. In the case of able-bodied young men like him, the Turks were striking first and asking questions never. Whenever the Turks were able to get the upper hand, they launched pogroms against both the Greek and Armenian communities. Pyotr had only gotten this far because others had spoken for him and miraculously had been believed.

He stirred restlessly, stifled by the long dress and all of the petticoats Katya had made him put on and by the heavy veil hiding—or at least he hoped hiding—his face. Katya was at his side again out on the crowded, open quay, holding him close to her, pretending that he was an ailing elderly woman relative, and doing everything she could to shield him from searching eyes that would recognize that he was not younger than eighteen nor older than forty-five and would mistake him for either Greek or Armenian. There was little reason for a young man of any other nationality to be here.

She had left his side soon after darkness had fallen over the milling crowd of refugees on the quay and as they were settling in for a summer of 1922 night when, yet again, no Greek ships had come into the harbor to start rescuing them. Pyotr knew what Katya was doing with the American relief service doctor in that waterfront building where the women in labor were being taken to give birth, and it drove him mad that she was doing it with the American and not him. But her connection with the American might be the only hope of survival for either one of them.

And he had no hold over Katya. She had never permitted him that close to her.

Because it was a pattern that had been going on for three nights, Katya was back at his side before midnight. Always at midnight, a great keening would go up across the packed harbor quay from the women camped out there. Most everyone out here was either a woman or a very young child or a very old man. None of the Greek and Armenian men who the Turks even suspected—in very broad terms—to be of military serviceable age were even let through the Turkish military's blockade of the inner harbor to wait for evacuation. Any such man was, instead, if not killed on the spot, being "marched inland," supposedly to holding camps, but in reality, just taken over the hills surrounding Smyrna, murdered, and shoveled into mass communal graves.

Each night the keening was met with the light of sweeping searchlights from the British, French, Italian, and American warships standing off from the harbor. Not knowing what was going on inside the harbor, the captains of the Allied ships believed that this sudden ghastly keening sound was some sort of mysterious phenomena that somehow could be quelled after several minutes by training the ships' searchlights on the quay. What the crews of these foreign naval vessels didn't realize about why their search lights were being successful in stopping the keening, however, was that the women in the crowds huddled on the quay were raising their voices in frightened chorus to stave off imminent danger.

This was the hour that raiding parties of the Turkish troops surrounding them were infiltrating the edges of the massed crowd of refugees. They were stealing onto the harbor quay to pull young woman—and sometimes boys—out of the mass and into the alleys behind their lines to have their way with them and then, with a flash of a knife, to thin out the "problem" of the Greeks and Armenians being "invited" to leave a now-liberated Turkey. The searchlights caused the soldiers to withdraw into their ranks, effectively meeting the keening women's goal, even though the crews of the Allied warships assumed flooding the docks with light was calming the frightened refugees down.

The keening hadn't started and yet both Pyotr and Katya sensed movement among the exhausted and sleeping groups of women, children, and infirm old men huddled around them. Katya pulled Pyotr close to her for mutual protection and they both barely were able to stifle their gasps as they realized that soldiers were stealing around the edges of the nearby groups, searching for prey. They had never come this far into the mass of the crowd before. Yet here they were. And they had seen that Pyotr—dressed as a woman—and Katya were awake, and were shrinking from them—and, in the dim light were more desirable and vulnerable than the other opportunities in the vicinity. There was no way that Katya could hide her beauty.

* * * *

Pyotr had marked his twenty-first birthday in late 1921 in the employ of the Greek merchant in various commodities, Theo Maneates. The Greek merchant lived with a wife, often absent in Athens, in a villa outside of Constantinople on a hill overlooking the Bosporus on the European bank of the city. When Pyotr moved into the small apartment over the stables, now turned into a garage for a big, black sedan, Maneates had a passage from the back hall of his villa to the garage enclosed with vine-covered trellising to mask his occasional nocturnal visits to Pyotr's rooms. In the more than a year that Pyotr lived there, as much in fact Maneates's chauffeur as in subterfuge, Pyotr settled into a life of relative comfort and security that he convinced himself was "enough."

If it were only Maneates, who made few demands on him in either transportation or the bed, in his life, Pyotr would probably have been discontent. But, first, there was the big, black town car Pyotr learned to drive and maintain and that continued to fascinate him and to be a matter pride, proving he actually had learned to do something useful in life.

And then there also was Kenneth O'Dell. Maneates insisted on paying Pyotr well, and Pyotr felt the guilt of being a Romanov enough that he passed on most of what he earned in some fashion or other to the Russian refugee community, which still was choking the streets, and to the relief efforts of the people of the diplomatic and relief agency community in Constantinople.

Theo Maneates was a devout Greek Orthodox Christian and he had a strict rule against going anywhere but church on Sunday, so, after driving Maneates home, Pyotr almost always was free for the rest of the day. One of the charitable tasks he fell into performing regularly then was going to Helen Bristol's refugee soup kitchen at the Sirkidji train station in Stambul and helping out on the serving line.

Another habit he thus fell into was to go to a nearby hotel with O'Dell after they had served the meal, in need of a man younger and more vigorous and attentive than Theo Maneates to make love to him for a couple of hours in the late afternoon.

So smitten with Pyotr was O'Dell that he was continually trying to pull Pyotr more and more into the social swirl of the diplomatic community.

"You are refined enough to pass as a Russian count, Pyotr," O'Dell whispered to him one afternoon. Pyotr turned his face around from his American lover so that he could hide the ironic smile that he could not quell.

"I am taking a sail next weekend on the Sea of Marmara with the Bristols on Admiral Bristol's flagship, *Scorpion*. Helen has seen you at the soup kitchen and more than once has invited you to come along. I'm sure Maneates will give you a couple of days off. I don't think you've had any time off since he engaged your services. What do you say?"

"I say it's very hard to act refined when you are laying on top of me with your cock buried deep inside me," Pyotr answered with a low laugh. He had been fending off similar invitations from O'Dell for months.

"I am being serious, Pyotr, and the Bristols need never know that I make love to you. I doubt that they know I make love to any man. The admiral can't see beyond his own nose, and I doubt that Helen cares. You've put off the invitation for some time. Helen Bristol will take offense, I think, if you continue doing so very much longer."

"I work, body and soul, for Theo Maneates. You know that, Kenneth. I can't be a chauffeur and lead a social life in the local diplomatic community as well. It's a false refinement that, you see—certainly not a social status that would accord me a place in your society."

"I don't think it is false refinement. You deport yourself as a member of the higher classes. Ask Maneates for permission. My guess is that he will be delighted to let you go on the cruise—for reasons of his own."

"I will ask, if you insist. But when he denies me permission, you must see that as reason to stop pressing me on the issue. And my guess at this very moment is that you are preparing to fuck me again, so there are far more pleasant things for us to be entertaining ourselves with than talking of class distinctions."

"That's a brilliant guess," O'Dell answered, as he wrapped his arms around Pyotr's chest and began the rhythm of the fuck inside him with a newly hardened staff.

As it turned out it was as O'Dell said, and Theo Maneates was delighted for Pyotr to become a cruise guest of the Bristols any time they wished. Bristol was the commander of the U.S. Black Sea Fleet and the senior American diplomat in Constantinople as well. And Maneates was a provisioner to the fleets when he could be. He was overjoyed at the prospect of getting an employee of his inside the Bristol inner circle, and from that time forward, Pyotr became a successful and influential salesman for Maneates as well as his chauffeur.

Helen Bristol was equally delighted with Pyotr, because he showed that he was, in fact, an expert bridge player. He also was easy on the eyes for Helen and the single women from the diplomatic and relief agency community who she invited on her cruises to even out the ratio of young naval officers and diplomats and young women. Both O'Dell and Maneates made certain that Pyotr had the right clothes to wear. Occasional near-starvation and the hard use of his body had kept him in a trim that matched his years at the Spartan military academy and that tailors clucked over in admiration.

They were sitting on the deck of the *Scorpion* one afternoon on the calm Sea of Marmara as O'Dell was showing his swimming prowess to the guests by swimming laps around the ship, when Helen leaned over to Pyotr while serving tea—Prohibition being in full force then so that harder liquor had to be served on one of the businessmen's yachts that sailed with the government-owned *Scorpion* and lashed to it during the evening to serve as a private bar—and said, "I hope the accommodations are not too cramped for you. You play a delightful hand of bridge, and I hope we will have you on a cruise again soon."

"The accommodations are just fine, Mrs. Bristol." Pyotr had to lift the teacup straightaway to his lips to keep from smiling. He was bunking with Kenneth O'Dell. So, the accommodations were delightful. He also was tempted to smile at the thought that O'Dell most probably would be having him again "soon" during the cruise.

Pyotr did so well with subtly selling Theo Maneates wares to the U.S. community through his connections with the Bristols and Kenneth O'Dell that by the spring of 1922, he no longer was Theo Maneates's chauffeur. He now was a trusted associate who Maneates wanted near him in his office. His remuneration improved, but only slightly, as the rich in Constantinople didn't maintain wealth by giving any more of it away than they had to. But it did mean that Pyotr had a bit more to give in charity to the Russian refugee community in the city that didn't seem to be decreasing any. Streams of White Russians continued to flow from the motherland, while only a trickle of refugees were leaving Constantinople for other lands.

Maneates's businesses included, quite prominently, importing of copperware from Turkey into Western Europe. This segment of his trade was so profitable that he had an office and a small townhouse in the Turkish harbor town of Smyrna on the Mediterranean. He visited this office for a couple of weeks two or three times a year. In the summer of 1922, he visited Smyrna—and he took his newly minted and highly trusted associate Pyotr Apraksin, with him.

Smyrna was governed by the Greeks at the time, the Greeks having taken advantage of Turkey being on the losing side of World War I by gaining a foothold on the Asian territory of Turkey and slowly expanding their land control. The Turks and Greeks had traditionally been at each other's throats back through time. Greece occupying Turkish territory had two major results—it caused the enmity between the two communities—and also the Turkish hatred for the more acquisitive and industrious ethnic group among them, the Armenians—to increase a hundredfold. And it also fomented a Turkish revolution in which upstart army officers under a colonel taking on the name Ataturk were well on the way to overthrowing the sultan of the rotting Ottoman Empire and creating a secular republic.

It was in the summer of 1922, when Theo Maneates took Pyotr to Smyrna, that the Turks defeated the Greek expansion and its army at Eskishehir. Within weeks Greek control of most of the Asian portion of Turkey, including in the city of Smyrna, had collapsed and the army retreated. Fast on the heels of their victory, the Turks, under the strong influence of Ataturk and his fellow army officers, were "inviting" Greeks and Armenians to emigrate immediately, and, increasingly, were forcing the issue with brutality.

But the Greeks and Armenians who did want to leave rather than be killed were not quickly able to do so. Once deciding they simply most go or die—albeit reluctant to do so because, under Turkish law, abandoned property vacated ownership—they fled, as possible, to coastal embarkation points. But initially there were no evacuation ships coming to pick them up. Greece didn't want them to abandon their foothold in Turkey. Warships of the other Allies that had defeated Turkey's side in the Great War, France, Italy, and England, as well as the naval contingent of the United States, which had not been at war with Turkey and thus wasn't formally among the occupying Allied forces, were near whatever troubles there were. But these contingents considered themselves there only as observers. Slowly they became embroiled in the evacuations of Greeks and Armenians from coastal towns, but only slowly and only as the brutality mobilized public opinion in Europe and North America—much quicker than it mobilized action in Athens.

To "help" the Greeks and Armenians leave, "someone" started fires in the Greek and Armenian quarters of Smyrna and started brutally herding women and young children and very old men to the inner harbor waterfront—and taking any male who could possibly take up arms out of the city, over the hill, and into mass graves.

When the fires started, Theo Maneates, a Greek, and Pyotr Apraksin, who quite easily could be mistaken for an Apollo-visaged Greek in the midst of chaos, were in Theo Maneates's residence above his offices and shop five blocks from the Smyrna inner harbor docks.

* * * *

Prior to these events, Pyotr found Smyrna in the early summer of 1922 even more inviting than he'd found Constantinople with its fast-paced life. He had always found it easy to pick up languages, having been in a household in St. Petersburg that spoke English and French fluently as well as Russian and where he'd even encountered German-speaking relatives on occasion. He'd studied both Latin and Greek in his childhood and exposure to Theo Maneates was honing his Greek and adding modern idioms to his vocabulary. He had also endeavored to pick up Turkish since he'd arrived in Constantinople, and here, in Smyrna, in the slower-paced environment, he was spending time in the back garden of Theo's townhouse improving his Turkish while watching the lithe, young Turkish gardener, Arief, bare-chested, sculpting a garden that had gone to the wild since Theo had last visited. As Arief worked, he and Pyotr bantered about in Turkish, with Pyotr's facility with the language improving daily. Theo was quite particular about having all of his properties kept trimmed, so Arief was working virtually full time during the day tending to the garden. Many of the evenings Arief was spending in Theo's bed on the third story of the small stone townhouse wedged in between other larger ones on a narrow street in the Greek quarter leading down to the Smyrna waterfront.

It was not that Theo was off Pyotr but, rather, that he liked variety and that the willowy, somewhat effeminate, dark Turk, Arief, was particularly arousing for a particular taste. Theo said that Arief, when swathed in veils and the candlelight of the night, reminded him of his wife when she was much younger and much less plump. Theo enjoyed fucking a young man dressed as a woman.

Pyotr also found Arief attractive—when he was working stripped down to his loin cloth in the garden—and Arief obviously was aroused by Pyotr, but Pyotr was not quite as much enticed with Theo's invitation to join the other two in the bedroom on the third floor. When Theo asked why this was so, wondering if it was the effeminate nature of Arief and the costumes of the night, Pyotr said that this wasn't the problem. He searched his brain for a reason even though he said he was unable to give Theo an explanation and decided that, indeed, he was not unaroused by the thought of fucking a transvestite. It was more that, when Pyotr observed the couplings, Arief played his role as an unwilling victim in these costume nights with Theo. It seemed to enhance Theo's ardor to play a game of taking Arief by force, with Arief playing the game because he was trying to please Theo. However, for some reason, this brought to Pyotr's mind how Mikhail had been passed around among the cadets in the academy barracks. Pyotr had had no particular trouble fucking Mikhail when the young man had begged for it—but he didn't find the group using Mikhail by right and without consultation arousing.

Pyotr assured Theo that he didn't find Arief unattracting, and it wasn't long before he proved that.

It was a sunny day in the back garden the afternoon that Pyotr fucked Arief. Much of the attraction of the small, dark-haired Turk was that he looked much like Pyotr recalled that Katya looked in the ways that attracted him so. Perhaps it was in the way he moved as he worked in the garden.

Pyotr was laying on his back, only in shorts, on a grassy patch beside a summer house hidden from view of the townhouse by tall bushes, and Arief, covered only by a loin cloth, was working on reweaving the vines of a rose bush on the trellising around the summer house. Arief was looking particularly provocative to Pyotr, whose shorts were tenting up and who was groaning inwardly at the effort not to give himself relief. As he worked Arief was drilling Pyotr on Turkish idioms.

Not being able to help himself and almost not realizing he had done so, Pyotr had moved a hand to his crotch and his voice, in responding to Arief's questions, had become thick and low. Arief stopped tugging at the vine and turned and looked at Pyotr.

"Why is it you stay away when old master invites you when I'm there in the night?" he asked. Pyotr could discern a bit of hurt in the young Turk's voice. He called Theo old master and Pyotr young master. "Do you not know I would wish you to be inside me too? Do you not know how I ache for you? Do you not find me attracting?"

"I find you particularly attracting, Arief. But I normally lay with Theo as you do with him. That is why I am here—why

92

Theo keeps me with him." This, in fact, was part of the reason Pyotr had not joined in a threesome, but he didn't want to tell Arief the main reason. He didn't want to spoil Theo's arousal in the arrangement that both he and Arief appeared to accept as satisfactory.

"But you don't always go with a lover that way, do you?"

"No . . . not always." Pyotr was thinking of Mikhail, and despite himself, he was being aroused. He encased his hard cock through the material of his shorts—he could not help himself from doing so.

"Please, let me do that." The voice was barely a whisper, but it came from very near. Pyotr opened his eyes to find Arief kneeling beside him. Arief laid a hand on Pyotr's belly. "Please," he repeated, almost plaintively.

Pyotr didn't answer, but he removed his hand from his crotch, and placed his arm around the kneeling Arief. His hand went to the small of Arief's back, just above where the crevice started, and he sighed and stroked Arief there as Arief's hand glided under his waistband and pushed Pyotr's shorts down to his knees. As Arief's mouth opened and slid down Pyotr's shaft, Pyotr groaned, dug his heels into the grass, and raised his pelvis, groaning again as the sensual fingers of Arief's hand wove into Pyotr's ball sack, separating and pulling the young Russian's testicles apart and gently rolling them with his fingers. Pyotr knew now why Theo groaned for Arief in the dark of the night in that other bedroom in ways that he didn't for Pyotr when he was giving the Greek suck.

Arief too groaned as Pyotr moved his hand across Arief's exposed buttocks cheeks where the loin cloth did not cover them and found and entered the young Turk's passage with his finger, searching for and finding the young man's prostate.

"Take me into the summer house, please. Now," Arief moaned when he pulled off the cock that had been stroking up into his mouth cavity from the leverage Pyotr was using off the heels of his feet in the grass.

Arief was begging for it, just as Mikhail had done. This was different from the role playing Theo and Arief engaged in in the night. For this, Pyotr was in high arousal.

93

Arief was bent over the rail at the back of the summer house on his belly, as Pyotr covered him close from behind, nibbled on his ear, and fucked him slowly and deep. Pyotr was mumbling as he fucked. Arief, lost in a world he had dreamed about ever since Pyotr had arrived in Smyrna, didn't pay attention to what Pyotr was mumbling beyond the occasional catch of a phrase referring to beauty and softness. If he had been listening, he most likely would have been curious why Pyotr was repeating the name "Katya."

After that, sometimes Theo fucked Arief in the night, before Arief went off to his own home somewhere in the Turkish sector of the city, and Pyotr fucked him during the day in the back garden. And more than once Pyotr responded to Theo's invitation to join Arief and him in Theo's chamber and Theo would watch Pyotr fucking Arief while Arief was expertly sucking Theo hard, whereupon Theo would come behind Pyotr and fuck him from behind, while Pyotr was fucking Arief.

To his shame, Pyotr found that, increasingly, he was able to become lost in the world of taking an unwilling, female Arief with as much lust as Theo did.

Theo occasionally mentioned the possibility of Pyotr and him fucking Arief together—and Arief showed no reluctance to doing this. But the occasion never arrived. This arousing threesome, satisfactory to them all, was short lived.

For several days after the results of the battle at Eskishehir reached the ears of those in Smyrna and loud praises to Allah were being almost continuously sung from the minarets in the Turkish section, there was no apparent change in the city. The surreptitious departure in the night of most of the Greek government officials and the movement into the streets of the Turkish soldiers that had been encamped nearby went largely unnoted by the populace, although what didn't go unnoticed was the subtle failure of some of the Greek and Armenian shops and cafés to open on expected mornings when they should be opened.

Theo Maneates, largely a stranger to the city, didn't notice the subtle differences occurring. Wholly unaccustomed to the ways of Turkish, Greek, and Armenian balancing in life, Pyotr made no note of it either. If the two were curious why

Arief simply did not appear for two days, they said nothing to each other, and both were so sexually exhausted from their most recent threesome that they each welcomed the respite. Theo might have noticed the paucity of business in his office downstairs and the absence of several of his Greek employees and nervous whisperings among the rest, but he was preoccupied with planning his near-term return to Constantinople.

Thus it was with some surprise that Pyotr ran across his former cadet friend, Mikhail Shevemetev, and his Turkish army captain sitting at a café table on the quay of the Smyrna waterfront. Pyotr knew that Mikhail and the Turk were somewhere about Smyrna, but the last Pyotr knew, the Turkish army was encamped outside the city and not permitted to enter it. Thus, he was surprised to see them.

Mikhail seemed even more surprised to see Pyotr here, because they had last met in Constantinople in circumstances that made Pyotr's presence in Smyrna highly unlikely. Still, it was Mikhail who saw and hailed Pyotr first. But Pyotr noted that his friend seemed somewhat disconcerted when Pyotr came over, greeting them, and asked if he could join them.

After a bit of "what brings you here?" chitchat in Turkish, Pyotr slowly started throwing in phrases in Russian until he'd been able to work up to a question in Russian that he wanted to ask Mikhail without Edom Yilmaz, the Turkish captain, understanding it. The Turk, other than looking hard at Pyotr from time to time, had had little to say, and Mikhail's reticence had not decreased. In fact, he increasingly looked like a scared rabbit. A wounded rabbit, as Pyotr could see some bruising on his small friend's face and at his neck.

"Is something wrong?" Pyotr asked in Russian, using a tone that would suggest that he wasn't saying anything serious. "You seemed scared—not completely happy to see me. While I can assure you that I'm very happy to see you again and to see that you are . . ." He almost said "all right," but he swallowed the end of that sentence, because Mikhail didn't really look all right. He was bruised and had lost weight. He looked gaunt.

"I had never expected to see you again," Mikhail whispered after a brief pause. "I'm sorry. I thought never to encounter you again."

"What is it?" Pyotr pressed.

"It's the captain," Mikhail said, obviously avoiding repeating the man's name. "He fancied you when he saw you in at the restaurant in Constantinople. He knew the waiters and waitresses were available. And he pressed me until I admitted that you and I had made love—and that you laid with the professor and let him have his way with you—that he took you rather than the other way around. The captain is only interested in taking."

"Yes, and?"

"He wants to fuck you too. He made me promise to arrange it if we ever met again."

They sat and looked into each other's eyes for a few moments. Pyotr could see the distress and fear—and genuine regret and concern—in Mikhail's eyes.

"Is it he who beat you?"

A pause and then, "Yes. It was not bad at first. Not when the Greeks had the upper hand here. But now that the Turks are taking over again, he has become more aggressive. And more cruel. I'm . . . I'm afraid that one day he will kill me. And there will be no one in authority here who cares if he does."

"Would it help you if I slept with him?"

Mikhail didn't answer at first. He just looked away, toward the gathering naval ships of the Allied nations on the horizon out to sea. But that, of course, was an answer to the question.

"Will it help?" Pyotr repeated.

"I can't ask you to do that. He is a cruel lover. He would bind you and use you roughly. I think he is obsessed with you. He has mentioned often that he wants to have you."

"I have known cruelty and rough taking," Pyotr answered in a low voice. He cleared his throat and turned his face toward the stony-aspected Turkish officer. "Mikhail tells me that you fancy me, Captain Yilmaz. Even before he said that, I was telling him what a handsome man you are, that I envied Mikhail, and that I wished I had someone handsome and virile like you to fuck me. And he told me that you are built like a stallion and might be interested. I know I am."

The captain inclined his head, gave a little grunt, and Pyotr could see a smile that was as much a sneer as a smile forming on his lips. He obviously was pleased by the flattery.

Mikhail broke in with a strangled voice. "But I don't think—"

"Mikhail tells me you like to fuck rough, a giving no quarter and taking-no-prisoners approach. I like that in a man," Pyotr said. "I want a man to show me he's a man. I want a man who will break me and use me to exhaustion. I think you might be that man. I think Turkish men dominate the best. I want to see you naked, to feel your teeth on my skin." Mikhail collapsed into his chair with a deep sigh of resignation, and Pyotr could see Yilmaz's eyes light up like a forest fire. A low growl was rising up from inside the Turkish soldier. Pyotr could see the man trembling, fighting hard to control himself from slamming Pyotr down on the café table top and having him right there.

How much worse could it be than it was with Nikolai, Pyotr wondered. He soon was to find out.

Pyotr was surprised to find out that Yilmaz had quarters right here in the city. He had assumed they would go to a hotel near the harbor—and that there would be a limited capability for bondage under such a situation. It wasn't until just now that Pyotr realized fully that the center of power in Smyrna had already changed. And as soon as they entered Yilmaz's bed chamber, Pyotr immediately understood the extent of the Turk's fetishes. Whips and chains were openly displayed on the chamber walls.

The bed was a four poster, with lengths of roping and leather restraints hanging off each post and from the center of the headboard. While Mikhail watched with concern from a chair nearby, Pyotr, naked, sat on the end of the bed, with Edom, naked, standing between his spread thighs, and Pyotr sucking his cock hard.

When the captain was ready, he roughly pulled Pyotr up to his feet, punched him in the mouth with a fist, which sent Pyotr flopping onto his back on the bed, stunned. Before Pyotr had come out of his haze from the surprise blow, Edom had tied his wrists together to the lead from the headboard over his head and was working on spreading and raising his legs and restraining them high on the posts at the foot of the bed.

He briefly used a whip on Pyotr until red welts had been raised on his chest, belly, and thighs. This made Yilmaz hard as a rock and his face contorted in a mask of lust and cruelty. Grabbing Pyotr's buttocks in a painful grip, the Turk raised the Russians pelvis to his throbbing cock, thrust deep inside him in one long slide, and fucked him hard to a prodigious, three-jerk ejaculation while he slapped Pyotr's face, chewed on his nipples, and beat him with fists on the torso and thighs. Pyotr gave him the mixed noises of hurting but still wanting Edom Yilmaz pounding inside him that he knew the Turk would find arousing.

When Pyotr was released, he surprised the captain by pushing him back on the surface of the bed, mounting the cock Pyotr had brought back to hard with his mouth, and riding him hard, throwing his head back and begging Yilmaz for the cock between gaggings from the rhythmic chocking Yilmaz was giving his neck.

When it was done and Yilmaz acknowledged it was the best sex—at least the best willing sex—he'd had in a long time and that he wanted to see Pyotr again, Pyotr took the initiative to say that he didn't think that Mikhail could withstand the taking that he could, and perhaps if Yilmaz was more gentle in fucking Mikhail, Pyotr would return to him as he wished.

The next night, Pyotr was awakened by the sound of angry voices in the floor below the bedrooms. He realized that it was light as day in the chamber as he rose from his bed, and then he could see through his window that the Greek quarter was on fire.

He was half way down the stairs when he was accosted by armed and angry Turks coming up toward him. They grabbed him with holds on his arms, legs, and nightshirt and dragged him down the stairs.

At the foot of the stairs, he recognized the sound of Arief, the gardener's voice, in high, panicked pitch.

"Not Greek, not Greek," he was crying out to the men manhandling Pyotr. "He is Russian. A Russian diplomat. Visiting

Smyrna and looking to buy goods. We must not. We must not. A friend. A buyer."

As quick as he had been seized, Pyotr was released and left in Theo's living room. All alone. Theo was nowhere to be found in the house. Arief was gone as well.

There was no sense of being in safety, however. Flames were dancing beyond every window. Pyotr raced upstairs to throw on some clothes and then down two stories and out into a narrow street clogged with screaming people running in every direction and being accosted here and there by bands of Turkish thugs.

* * * *

Pyotr stumbled down the smoke-filled street, headed toward the harbor. It seemed that that was where Arief had screamed at him to go, before the young gardener was swept out of Theo's house with the bloodthirsty band of Turkish vigilantes. He wondered if Theo had already gone there, although even while he thought about it, he'd realized that this wasn't the case. He'd heard Theo's screams. That had been what had awakened him. And he saw the blood on the living room carpet as he was struggling with the Turkish hoodlums. There was too much blood there.

This couldn't be happening. But it *was* happening. And it was happening all around him. Out of the swirls of smoke, Pyotr saw tragedy all around him. He moved as if in a separate, surreal world. No one had accosted him—yet—but he wasn't so delusional that he had any faith he'd ever make it to the harbor alive. Here there was a middle-aged man, clutching a canvas bag to his chest, protecting it, even as he was surrounded by Turkish youths—not more than boys, really—beating him to a pulp with clubs. On the other side of the street, even as Pyotr cleared by the first tableau, there were other Turks, with knives, who had cornered an elderly woman. Pyotr saw the gleam of the golden rings on her hands as she threw them up to block the look of horror on her face—and then, as he stumbled past, he saw the flash of a knife and her disembodied hand hit the cobblestones, as the Turks crouched down to retrieve the gold rings. Further on, a family was struggling down the road, and Pyotr heard the scream of one of their young daughters being snatched and pulled into an alley. A man stopped in his tracks and turned to the alley, with the rest of the family scurrying ahead. He didn't reach the opening to the alley before he disappeared under a pile of bodies slashing at him with clubs and knives.

The young Russian himself didn't make it too much further before he ran into the back of a horse-drawn cart with a thin, Western-clothed man atop flicking a whip and repeatedly yelling "American relief doctor; make way" in broken Turkish.

Amazingly, everyone in the street was making way for the cart. Pyotr was about to try to move around it when the canvas sacks at the back of the cart were raised far enough for him to see a face of an angel appear and two thin arms reaching out toward him. A voice was crying out, "Pyotr. Here. Climb under here. Quickly."

And numb from surprise and shock, Pyotr felt Katya Betskoya drawing him into the cart and pulling canvas sacking over his body.

* * * *

"I don't know how the Petrosians are faring," Katya answered. "I fear the worst. Gurgen saw what was happening in Sevastopol and had his own ship there. We sailed a few days before the Bolsheviks invaded the Crimea and came here, to Smyrna, where Gurgen had family and part of his business in the Armenian quarter."

"I was with Samuel at the American relief agency camp when the fires, killing, and looting started in the Armenian quarter. I couldn't go back to the Petrosians' house, and Samuel was coming down to the harbor to open a clinic in a house down on the harbor and said it was best if I came with him. I have been helping at his clinic and he said this was where the help would be needed."

Pyotr and Katya were sitting off to the side of where the American doctor, Samuel Covington, and the aid workers who had already arrived at the small house opening directly onto the Smyrna quay were setting up cots and examination and treatment stations. Each of the relief workers wore a badge of safe passage with their name, age, and gender penned on them, issued by the Turkish army, to give them whatever safety was possible in the pandemonium around them. Katya had such a badge. There was none for Pyotr.

As yet there were no refugees who had found a clinic was opening in the harbor, although the wailing that could be heard from beyond the stone walls of the house indicated that crowds of frightened and wounded Greeks and Armenians were already arriving at the quay and it would not be long before the clinic would be swamped with business.

Katya had brought food and water to Pyotr and had said she could sit with him for a few minutes before she was needed. She listened calmly to Pyotr's explanation of why he too was in Smyrna and the two spoke of the coincidence of circumstances that had brought them together again—and avoided talking about the probable fate of the Petrosians and Theo Maneates.

Samuel Covington came over to them as Pyotr was finishing the simple meal Katya had given him. Pyotr and the American doctor had already met briefly, and Covington was more focused on Katya now than on the young Russian who had suddenly appeared and with whom, Covington had been told in brief terms, Katya shared some sketchy past.

As Covington and Katya conversed quietly about preparations for the onslaught of patients, Pyotr had time to look the American over. There was familiarity between the two that warned Pyotr that their relationship wasn't a casual—or even just a professional—one. The American doctor was tall and thin, wore glasses that apparently he would be nearly blind without, and had sandy-colored hair and a receding hairline. He seemed both patrician and severe in aspect and clearly was on edge from the great responsibility facing him within hours.

"We all need to get some sleep, for as long as we can," Pyotr heard Covington say to Katya in a louder voice than he had been speaking to her in as Pyotr gave him the once over.

"There are rooms upstairs, Pyotr," Katya said. "The cots there will be needed by patients soon enough, but you should take one in the room at the back of the building until it is needed. We also will need to think of some way to keep you safe but away from here until you can board one of the evacuation boats that should arrive at any time."

"Some way to keep me safe?" Pyotr asked.

"Yes. The Turks are unlikely to pay much attention to whether you are Russian rather than Greek or Armenian, and they are taking away all Greek and Armenian men of serviceable age. Samuel tells me the Turkish authorities will be searching through this building every couple of hours to ensure we aren't harboring any Greek or Armenian men. You have no badge, so there is no protection for you here—and not much for the rest of us if the Turks think we are harboring a fugitive. It won't be safe for you to be out on the quay either without some sort of disguising of your age and gender. I will try to think of something. For now, try to get some sleep and gather your strength."

Pyotr went to the room as assigned and slept fitfully enough that not more than an hour later he heard the sounds from the room to the front of the building—sounds that were familiar. Without thinking he rose from his cot and moved quietly out into the hallway and to the slightly open door of the room at the front.

By all rights he should have been shocked and angry and disillusioned all at once, but his life so far had become so taken up in turmoil and his attraction to Katya was so strong that, other than being surprised, he did not lose any of the ardor he had for her.

Katya was on her back on the edge of the cot, her skirt-covered legs reaching to the floor, and Samuel Covington, thin, wiry-muscled, naked and in full arousal, was crouched over her. She was nestled in one of his arms and his other one was up under the front of her skirt, up to his elbow. From the rustling movement of the material of Katya's skirt, Pyotr could tell that Covington was working the center of her. His face was plastered to hers and they were kissing deeply and moaning almost in harmony. As Pyotr watched, Covington pushed Katya's skirt up to her waist, exposing her well-turned calves, thighs, and naked pelvis. Pyotr gave a little cry, which the couple didn't hear above their own sounds of lustful arousal, and sank to the floor, his eyes wide and unable to look away. Covington was masturbating

Katya's cock, which was hard and long. Nothing could pull Pyotr's attention away from seeing the cock on Katya. He remained, collapsed on the floor, as their lovemaking continued and climaxed. There was no question that Covington knew who and what he was coupling with—or that he too was in high arousal, his cock, not as long as Katya's, curving up in a hard arc from his groin. The American lowered his head to Katya's belly, and to her audible sigh, opened his mouth over her shaft and slowly descended on it as she began a slow, rhythmic thrusting of her slim hips and reached for and encased Covington's shaft in her small fist.

At the moment of penetration, Samuel Covington was laying on his stomach on the cot, with his hands dragging the floor on either side and his head lolled to the side. The expression on his face was one of ecstasy, and he was panting hard and moaning in a low drone. Katya, her skirts gathered up around her waist and her legs and hips naked, straddled Samuel's hips and began fucking him in long, deep, masterful thrusts. Katya's balls were slapping against Samuel's buttocks cheeks in a tattoo that sounded like jabs of a shovel in mud to Pyotr's ears. The man was groaning and grunting and writhing under her, begging her to fuck deeper and faster, as she reached back through his thighs, pulled his cock through, and pumped it with her fist. There was no question who mastered who. The act of Katya fucking the American sent a current of electricity through Pyotr's body.

Where one day there may have been disbelief and disgust, Pyotr now, once the shock had passed, only felt arousal and the wish that Katya would be fucking him like the transvestite was fucking the American doctor. After Katya arched her back, gave a little cry, ejaculated inside the doctor, and collapsed on his back. Covington turned his face to hers and the two were kissing deeply, Pyotr gathered himself up from the floor in front of the door, returned to his cot in the other room, and masturbated himself to a fitful sleep in which he dreamed of Katya doing to him what she had done to the American doctor. There had been no question that the American had thoroughly enjoyed the coupling, nor that he was under Katya's full control.

On the morrow, Pyotr found that Katya's plan for him was to dress him in women's clothes—which gave him a little thrill of being as close to her emotionally as possible—and to send him out on the quay to wait, in disguise, with the women, young children, and old men out there in the hope of getting on an evacuation ship—if and when they arrived in the harbor.

Katya spent as much time as she could out there with him to help him avoid contact with other people who might discover he wasn't a woman. And thus it came to be that they were there together, at midnight, the night that a Turkish unit of soldiers raided into the crowd in search of women, girls, and boys to kidnap, defile, and send off into another world.

Two soldiers saw the beautiful Katya and each leaned down and grabbed an arm and started to pull her in two different directions. A third arrived and started to organize an effort to pull her toward the edge of the crowd. Other refugees were stirring, and the women were beginning to keen their warning of the presence of vultures. Pyotr leaped up and grabbed the men who were struggling with Katya. He managed to break their hold enough that Katya pulled free and melted into the crowd as the searchlights from the Allied naval vessels started to pan over the crowd.

The soldiers piled on Pyotr and manhandled him toward the edge of the crowd and the dark shadows of the buildings bordering the open quay. They had not yet discovered that he wasn't a young woman. As they got to the edge of the crowd and the opening of a road up into the Turkish quarter, though, an officer appeared, barked orders, and the soldiers released Pyotr and evaporated into the shadows. They had ripped away enough of Pyotr's clothing, though, that he was revealed to be a young man.

Other soldiers stepped forward prepared to take hold of him and start his way into the afterlife as they were doing with all other Greek and Armenian men of his age, when the officer barked orders again.

The officer was Captain Edom Yilmaz. He took possession of Pyotr, marched him up into the Turkish quarter in a quick step to his quarters, where he pushed Pyotr up the stairs to his bed chamber, bound him firmly to the bed, whipped him into whimpering submission, and fucked the stuffing out of him.

* * * *

"Pyotr, thank god you're alive. But we haven't much time. The Turk could come back at any moment."

Pyotr struggled to open his eyes. Both were swollen from the beating the captain had given him while he fucked him over the hours—Pyotr had no idea how many. He was still tied to the bed, but Katya, Mikhail, and the American doctor were each at a corner, cutting the bounds away with knives.

"Wha . . .?" was the best that Pyotr could manage. He was bruised and in pain in every muscle.

"Shhh, conserve your strength," Katya hissed. "I saw you being taken away and I sent one of the Turkish relief workers to follow you. The clinic has been closed down. The Turks see no need to give health care to the refugees on the quay; they'd prefer all of the refugees died. Samuel will take us back to the encampment in the cart. An American destroyer is off the coast there to evacuate the relief team, and Samuel is saying that you, Mikhail, and I are part of the team."

She paused and looked down at Pyotr's face. It was evident to Pyotr that she expected him to ask why the American would do this for her. But Pyotr knew why. He didn't ask, and he didn't judge. He only envied. Instead, he mumbled, "Mikhail too?"

"Yes, he's going with us. The American ship will take us all back to Constantinople. Now don't exert yourself further; you'll need what's left of your strength for the journey under sacks in the cart."

Chapter Seven: Constantinople Redux

Moaning was Pyotr's only defense against the glorious onslaught, He was gripping the thin coverlet on the bed in both his fists and teeth. He was crouched over the side of the bed, his legs spread and his bare toes digging into the wood of the floor. His cock had been pulled back between his legs, and it, his balls, and his entrance were being assaulted by expert lips and tongue and scraping teeth until, in a groan of surrender, he came in a fountaining of cum. Only then, after Pyotr had been completely satisfied did the American diplomat stand, hunch over his back, grab his legs in a wheelbarrow stance, press the head of his skin-sheathed cock inside Pyotr's channel, and worry Pyotr's prostate with it until Pyotr came again. Then and only then, when Pyotr was completely spent, did Kenneth O'Dell turn Pyotr on his cock so that the young Russian faced him. Propping Pyotr's ankles on his shoulders, he began pumping Pyotr fast and deep so that Pyotr gasped and panted and writhed under the older, larger man and cried out how much he wanted exactly what he was getting.

No man who Pyotr had ever lain under fucked him as fully and satisfyingly as Kenneth O'Dell did. And no one was capable of taking him so lovingly either. He varied his fucking.

One day, he'd be rough and overpowering; another day he'd be gentle and solicitous of Pyotr's every need and wish. Pyotr called no favorite; O'Dell could do whatever he wished with him, and he would melt to it as he never had done for any other man.

As both lay on the bed exhausted, O'Dell repeated the plea that he had made each Sunday for the past four weeks.

"This is no mere dalliance, Pyotr. I'm sure not for you any more than it is for me. You body doesn't lie to me. I'm being assigned back to the States in the spring. You can come with me. You must come with me. Surely you want to leave Constantinople. I can make a new life for you—for us—in the States. But I must start the paperwork soon if it is to happen smoothly."

Pyotr sighed with regret as he'd done each previous time. "I cannot come with you. I've told you that before. Nothing has changed."

"But why? You've never given me a good reason why. Don't you want me? Is it that you cannot lay with just one man? I will share you if that's what you must have. I'll do anything to make you happy."

"You know it's not that," Pyotr said, turning and running his fingers over O'Dell's jaw line and then leaning in to him and giving him a kiss. "You do everything to make me happy. I just can't leave Constantinople and go with you."

And Pyotr couldn't tell him why he couldn't. He did love O'Dell above almost all others. But he couldn't go with him to the States as long as there was a chance for him and Katya.

Even though life would inevitably be changed in the spring when Kenneth O'Dell left Constantinople, for now it was almost as if Smyrna had never happened. Pyotr was back in Constantinople, working now as manager of Theo Maneates's Turkish interests—until, Theo's wife in Athens said, Theo returned from Smyrna. Of course, though they wouldn't say it, neither Pyotr nor Theo's wife really thought that ever would happen. He was still being paid a pittance, but he had status now. And that was much harder for a Russian refugee to achieve in Constantinople than money.

Pyotr had also returned to helping on Sunday afternoon in Helen Bristol's Russian refugee soup kitchen at the Sirkidji train station in Stambul. Although nearly two years after the initial influx most of the faces of the Russian refugees had changed, because many of the original evacuees had managed to go on to other countries and new lives, White Russian refugees were still flowing out of Russia via the Black Sea and washing up on Constantinople's docks.

Kenneth O'Dell was still working at the soup kitchen on Sunday afternoons as well, and thus O'Dell was still taking Pyotr to a Horhor Street hotel after their shift was over and fucking him to heaven. What was new was that the quality of the hotel they used had improved and O'Dell was now using the skin condoms he preferred and brought himself rather than the latex ones the hotel had initially provided. O'Dell had suggested that they forgo the condoms altogether, but Pyotr had correctly seen that as a subtle attempt by O'Dell to solidify their relationship and make it monogamous. That was when Pyotr had said he could not commit to being only with O'Dell. Although at the time Pyotr had been afraid that O'Dell would then leave him, such was his control over the American diplomat that he said he would live with Pyotr's decision. Pyotr wasn't fucking other men, though. In his mind, however, he was still available to Katya whenever she wanted him, so he couldn't bring himself to pledge total commitment to O'Dell. He could not bring himself to tell the American this.

Just as before, Pyotr was being invited to the Bristols' weekend cruises in the admiral's flagship, *Scorpion*, when they invited Kenneth O'Dell, and Pyotr usually accepted the invitation. Now nearly everyone pretty much knew—but didn't say—that O'Dell and Pyotr were a pair. But as long as both were handsome and witty and played an expert hand of bridge, Helen Bristol didn't care what they did in their shared cabin. The admiral possibly would have cared if he'd known, but he was much too busy, as the senior U.S. diplomat in Constantinople, not knowing—or, more accurately, turning a blind eye to—what was going on in Turkey to know what was going on inside his wife's weekend cruise parties.

O'Dell and Pyotr also were being openly seen in each other's company in Constantinople restaurants and nightclubs. Pyotr no longer was a chauffeur but now was the Turkey manager for the Maneates holdings, a major provisioner of the U.S. missions in Turkey. So it wasn't out of keeping for the two men to fraternize in public.

It was during one such meal together, at the expatriate community restaurant and night club, Moscovite, that Pyotr was to see something he was always to remember later.

"Who is that extraordinary-looking man at the table over there with those six children?" he asked Kenneth. He had brought O'Dell's attention to a chunky, middle-aged man in a U.S. naval admiral's uniform sitting at a table with six children of various sizes gathered around him. The man had gray hair in abundance but was sporting a black handlebar mustache. "The man is obviously American, but the children all look Russian and he must be old enough to be their grandfather. I didn't realize that the Moscovite served children this late in the evening."

"Who?" O'Dell asked, tearing his attention away from the tough chicken breast he was wrestling with and looking in the direction in which Pyotr's fork was pointing. "Oh him. That's Admiral Newton McCully. He's such a commanding figure here that the Moscovite would serve goats if they pattered in here by his side."

"Not the Admiral McCully of the Crimea evacuation?" Pyotr declared.

"The same," O'Dell answered.

Pyotr looked back at the admiral with renewed respect. McCully was a legend in the region and a hero to the Russian evacuees. As the American observer to the White Russian army in the Black Sea region, McCully had pressed—over Bristol's objections even—for American involvement in the evacuation from the Crimea before anyone else had seen the need. He had eventually prevailed, and the ships under his command, the cruiser *USS Galveston* and destroyer *Smith Thompson* were in the forefront of the Allied forces participation in that evacuation, making trip after trip between Sevastopol and Constantinople until the Bolshevik army had overrun the city.

"But the children?" Pyotr said. "Is there a story there?"

"There certainly is. It's the talk of the American consulate. He rescued those children one by one from dire circumstances in the evacuation of Sevastopol, and he insists that he's personally adopting them all and taking them back to America when he is transferred there. And he's not even married. Bristol is livid. He says if he lets McCully do it, others will want to do it too. And McCully answered with a 'so what?' There's quite a struggle going on over that, but knowing McCully and how tenacious he was with the need for the United States to be involved early in the Crimea evacuation, I'll bet he finds a way to get those children to America. He'll probably just sail home with them."

"More power to him," Pyotr said in a small voice. He felt choked up—and it wasn't from the tough chicken the Moscovite was serving that evening.

In a move that Pyotr was to remember later, O'Dell carefully put his eating utensils down next to his plate, wiped his mouth with his napkin, took a hard look at Pyotr, and said, "Then you don't disapprove of an American adopting a Russian refugee to enable him or her to go to America?"

"No, I think what McCully is trying to do is admirable. If those children make it to the States, I'm sure they will be among the luckiest Russians to have survived this debacle. And it demonstrates how much more the Americans have done for my people than any other nation has. If there ever is another tsar, he must give that man a medal."

O'Dell smiled a small smile, inclined his head briefly, picked up his fork and knife, and once more attacked the unyielding chicken breast, which he'd complain about if those eating at the Moscovite weren't enjoying far better fare than most across Constantinople were, and in particular those in the Russian refugee camps in Stambul and on the Isle of Proti.

* * * *

Pyotr no longer lived in the refugee camp, or on the streets, or even at an establishment such as Martin's Tea Room. He now shared a garret apartment in a building of other Russian expatriates doing at least slightly better than most, with Mikhail and, when she wasn't with the American relief doctor, Samuel Covington, with Katya Betskoya. The three had become almost inseparable—like brothers and sister—ever since they had

111

escaped Smyrna together on a U.S. destroyer at the behest of Covington. At least that was how Katya saw the relationship. Having seen Katya fucking Covington and still wishing it was him, Pyotr had great trouble being satisfied with a brother-sister relationship. Mikhail just seemed happy to be free of his Turkish captain again.

Both Mikhail and Katya worked on the wait staff at the Parizen restaurant. Both supplemented their incomes by going with restaurant clients when asked, with Katya's regular clientele being even more select than Mikhail's, and Katya was still servicing Covington a couple of times a week. But since the horrendous experience they'd all lived through in Smyrna, none of them had had sex with each other.

Pyotr ached to couple with Katya, even more now than before he knew she was a transvestite, but Katya never took the hints of interest he gave no matter how specific they were. Pyotr suspected that Katya didn't know he was aware of her secret and that for some reason it was important to her that he not know. He was conflicted over whether to tell her he did or not—and that it made no difference to him or the strength of his ardor. He was afraid of how she would react if he told her he knew.

He was determined that someday he would gather the strength to talk to her about it—and then to get across to her how much he ached for her. But that "someday" never seemed to come. He didn't want to possess her; he wanted her to possess him, just as he'd seen her mastering Covington.

He suspected that Katya knew that he was really—or once had been—a Romanov count. She may have remembered remarks casually dropped by others back on the evacuation ship to Sevastopol. Mikhail knew, of course, but Pyotr had sworn him to secrecy and was confident that Mikhail had said nothing. But the woman in the apartment on the first floor, rear of their apartment house, the Countess Demidova, had recognized him. He had denied he was a Romanov—and, specifically, the man she knew him to be—and she had dropped the effort to get him to acknowledge that he was who she believed him to be. But she was somewhat demented now, living in poverty off the seamstress earnings of a faithful servant who had escaped from Russia with her when she was marked for execution by the

Bolsheviks, even though the countess had spent her entire life in charity work for the poor. The poor woman thought they were living on her own vanished wealth. Pyotr knew that she and Katya talked, and he was afraid that Katya knew who he was and was avoiding coupling with him not only to maintain the ruse that she was equipped as a woman should be but also because Pyotr was too royal for her.

He realized he was following a double standard. While he wanted Katya to know nothing about him, he wanted to know everything about Katya—about how she had come to be like she was. For a fleeting moment one morning in early fall, he thought he might be able to make those discoveries without prying them from her.

He was perusing the bookstalls along the Vatan Coddese when he ran across a novel by Katya's father, Fydor Betskoy. It was in Russian and the title of the novel, *Demytri, My Son*, struck Pyotr. He remembered that many of Betskoy's novels were reputed to be largely autobiographical. He picked the book up from the bin and turned it over and over in his hand, excited at the prospect that it would have revelations in it about Katya. He wracked his brain trying to remember whether Katya had ever said she had brothers.

He heard a voice behind him, on the street, calling out "Count Pyotr," though, and he dropped the book in surprise and turned toward the voice, instantly wanting to hush it up. It was Boris, the old servant of his distant cousin, Prince Toubetskoy. He was about to say something dismissive to the servant, when the old man broke in.

"I've been looking for you everywhere. The prince has urgent news he wishes to share with you and has sent me out to seek you."

Forgetting all else, Pyotr bade Boris show him the way and fought to control his own steps so that he didn't rush the tottering old man beyond his endurance.

The room was dark, and the prince, if anything, looked closer to the grave than to life.

"It is tragic news—for both of us—Pyotr," the prince said in a low, rasping voice. "But I knew you would not want to go through life with the uncertainty. And soon, I would not be able to tell you what I have been told."

"You are not well, Cousin?" Pyotr asked, thinking that health must surely be the issue.

With slight irritation, though, the prince waved the question off. "No, I am quite well, thank you. No, I am leaving to live in Paris soon—and I will do so as soon as I can find a young companion to carry the burdens of going there. Boris is older than I am, and I'm afraid he's well passed handling such a responsibility."

"Is that why you've called me?" Pyotr asked. "You want me to take you to Paris?"

"I may give you that privilege as a last resort, Pyotr, but I'm rather hoping that a younger, smaller man than you will be my companion. It seems I will not be permitted to travel with one as young as I like, so I suppose I am left with the need for youthful appearance."

Pyotr looked into the old goat's eyes and saw that he was quite serious about this. Would he never give up his proclivities? Pyotr wondered.

"So, why have you . . . ? Oh, are you saying that you want me to procure a young man for you? Younger and more boyish then me, I take it?"

The prince just sat there, looking meaningfully at Pyotr, somewhat as a parent would at a child who wasn't understanding the obvious.

"And is this the momentous reason you had Boris search the streets of Constantinople for me?"

"It is just a side issue." The prince paused and turned his head away. When he looked back at Pyotr, his expression was a softer one, one of sadness, and he simply said, "They are all dead, Pyotr."

"I beg your pardon."

"Your family. None but you left St. Petersburg. They were all murdered by the Bolsheviks before you ever left Russia. They were too slow, too trusting of those around them, to leave in time. You need to know that. The tsar and his family are gone too. Rumors are already rife that one of the daughters—and the tsarevitch—somehow survived and were spirited away. But I'm sure that's all politics. The Bolsheviks have proven to be more organized than to let that happen. That era is over. Mother Russia as we knew is dead. Of that, I'm sure."

Pyotr sat, stunned. He'd always supposed that most of the family had been killed, but surely at least one of them . . .

"As long as you are here, perhaps you will indulge a favorite relative again."

Pyotr looked to his side, where the prince was sitting very close to him in his wheelchair, his lap blanket on the floor at his side and his cock out and being held in one hand. His other hand was unbuttoning Pyotr's fly.

Still in shock, Pyotr just leaned back in his chair and let what would be be.

He had the presence of mind to go back to the book stall where the prince's servant had found him after he had given the old fossil what he wanted—but look as he might he couldn't find the novel again by Fydor Betskoy about a son. And when he queried about the book to the bookstall owner, the look he received was as if he was hallucinating that such a book or author ever existed.

* * * *

It was twilight on a Sunday. Pyotr and Kenneth O'Dell had worked their shift in Helen Bristol's soup kitchen and, as usual, had retired to a hotel for a session of lovemaking. Once again O'Dell had asked Pyotr to go to the States with him and once again Pyotr had answered that he could not do that.

"But you saw Admiral McCully with those children the other evening—that he intends to adopt them. That's a way to get to America, Pyotr. I'm offering to adopt you."

"You aren't old enough to be my father."

"McCully is old enough to be those childrens' grandfather. And he isn't married either. I'm a decade older than you are. There's no reason for anyone to think that I can't be a father figure to you—even with them secretly understanding that I'm doing no less than McCully is doing. That I am saving Russians, one person at a time."

"I still cannot go with you. I can't leave Constantinople yet. I love you for the offer, but please don't press me further."

Showing his sadness and his frustration, O'Dell had washed himself off and quickly departed while Pyotr was still feeling too weak from the fucking to rise from the bed. He heard the door to the room open, though, and he turned to speak.

"Have you forgotten—?"

He only had time to rise, naked, from the bed in surprise and consternation, though, when a fist blow to his belly, followed by an uppercut to his chin sent him reeling back onto the bed.

"So, you are still at it, are you?" Nikolai Saltykov growled. He was unbuttoning and dropping his tightly tailored sailor's trousers. "I saw you lure that older fancy man to this hotel. I want some of what you gave him. And, seeing that we are old friends, you will be happy to give it to me for free."

"Nikolai, don't." Pyotr cried out. But Nikolai punched him again, snapping Pyotr's head back to where it cracked against the wall on the other side of the bed. Dazed, he lay there defenseless, as Nikolai jerked his legs apart and started to fuck him furiously.

Resigned to the fucking as he always had had to be with Nikolai, Pyotr turned his head to the headboard and threw an arm over his face both to protect his head from Nikolai's blows, albeit belatedly, and also so that he couldn't see the anger in Nikolai's eyes in the taking. It was no easier to see even with the realization that it wasn't personal—that Nikolai, by his origins, was no less contemptuous of the tsar's class than any of the Bolsheviks now ruling in Russia and tracking down and degrading and murdering any royal they could find.

He heard Nikolai give a cry and fall forward on top of him in heavy, lifeless weight, though, and his eyes flew open. The first images he saw were the surprised look on Nikolai's face and then the burst of blood flowing out of the former academy cadet's mouth. The second image, swimming up over Nikolai's collapsed torso was of the wild eyes of Mikhail.

"Mikhail! What have you done?" Pyotr cried out.

"I saw Nikolai following you and the American and I followed him to see if he would make mischief."

116

The knife Mikhail was holding in his hands was covered in Nikolai's blood.

Recovering quickly, as he knew he had to, Pyotr sent Mikhail to check the nearby rooms for one with an unlocked door and no occupant, while he did his best to contain the bleeding of Nikolai's body. Together they moved the body to an unoccupied room, exchanged the bed linens, and did what they could to clean up any evidence of where the murder had occurred.

Only when they were down the stairs and out onto the street did they feel free either to take a deep breath or to speak.

"What is to become of me?" Mikhail whimpered.

"You did what you had to do, and you did it for me," Pyotr answered. "I don't think you will be connected to the killing. But we can't chance it. The Turks would not be sad to summarily execute a Russian murderer. They would be especially happy that the victim was Russian too. Two fewer burdens to worry about."

"What is to become of me?" Mikhail repeated.

At that moment Pyotr realized that Mikhail would not be able to keep the deed secret. He was quaking, had vomited in the gutter as soon as they had vacated the hotel, and was muttering to himself almost as a madman.

Mikhail would have to go farther away than to the apartment they shared.

Taking a firm grip on Mikhail's arm, Pyotr said in a commanding voice that cut through the small, young Russian's meltdown, "Come with me, Mikhail. You are moving to Paris with a randy old goat of a Russian prince."

* * * *

Through the cold winter of 1922, Pyotr tried to tell Katya how he felt about her. But she would have none of it. He had thought that, with Mikhail gone and well settled now—as a letter from Paris had announced that the prince had formally adopted Mikhail and made him heir to a still-sizeable fortune—it might be different in their apartment with just the two of them. But not even when their breaths were fogged in the ice-cold, unheated room on the coldest nights of the deepest winter was Pyotr able to get Katya to bundle with him so that he might have a start of melting her heart and resolve.

Katya was kind and affectionate to him—but in the way a sister would be to a brother.

Pyotr did manage to tell Katya of his feeling for her and that it didn't matter whatever secret she was keeping from him—that he would still love her. But when he did this, she just looked sad and said their time had never had a chance—that she was serious about the American relief doctor, Samuel Covington now. She even remonstrated with Pyotr a bit, reminding him that he, as well as Katya, owed his deliverance from Smyrna to the American doctor.

She never came anywhere close to telling Pyotr that she was really a he, a transvestite who was a woman only in terms of the beauty and illusion of femininity she could create with cosmetics and the clothing she wore and the studied movements she made.

And thus, Pyotr had not been able to tell her that it didn't matter a bit to him. That he loved and was loved by men too—and that he wanted her inside him if that was how she expressed her love. It was how he'd seen her having sex with the American doctor.

The American doctor obviously knew what she was, and if they were still coupling, Pyotr felt the disadvantage he had against a man who was having and enjoying what Pyotr could not attain.

The day came when Pyotr found that nothing stays the same forever and that his chances with Katya had slipped out of his hands.

One night he came back to the apartment and Katya wasn't there. And she wasn't there in the morning either. He checked at the Parizen restaurant only to be told she hadn't worked there in weeks. He went to the American relief agency, but no one would tell him where the American doctor, Samuel Covington, lived.

On the third night of Katya's absence, a Saturday, the nearly demented Countess Demidova in the apartment on the

118

first floor back remembered that Katya had left and given her a note to give to him.

> *I have gone to America with Samuel, which is the right thing to do for a man who saved us and wants me as I am. I would have had you by preference, but I cannot hurt you because of what I am. I am still a daughter of Russia; I could not live up to you and your family.*

Pyotr read the note over and over, tears streaming from his eyes over what he had lost by not forcing the issue.

The next day, as Pyotr was standing beside Kenneth O'Dell and they were serving the tired- and defeated-looking line of White Russian refugees shuffling through the food line of Helen Bristol's soup kitchen, Pyotr leaned over and whispered to O'Dell, "Do you still wish me to come to the States with you?"

"Yes, of course," the American diplomat answered, almost dropping his serving spoon in surprise.

"Then I will do so," Pyotr answered. "I will want a new life, though. In America, I will be Peter, but I will need a new last name. I must change. With each step toward a new life, I must be a new person."

"It will be simpler if you take my name—if I formally adopt you. Is there any reason now why I cannot adopt you?"

Pyotr's thoughts went to Mikhail and Pyotr's awful old cousin, Prince Toubetskoy. Mikhail had written that he was happy being the prince's son. That everything was taken care of and that the prince only made one demand on him—one that was easily given considering what Mikhail had been through in life.

Thinking on what Kenneth O'Dell gave him, Pyotr considered that being adopted by a man he could then more openly live with—a man as vigorous and attentive as O'Dell—should be so much more satisfactory than even Mikhail's situation had become.

"Of course, I would like that," Pyotr answered. And then, thinking not only of Kenneth's devotion but also the years it might take for him to ever see Katya again, he added, "And if you are still interested, I suggest that we dispense with those skin condoms now. I am ready for the commitment that requires."

The look that O'Dell gave him almost sent Pyotr into tears in reflection of the selfishness with which he had been treating the man who had given him so much without demands in return.

* * * *

Late in the next spring Peter O'Dell stood at the rail of a passenger liner beside his "father," Kenneth, as the great ship pulled away from a Constantinople dock and into the Sea of Marmara en route to New York City.

Peter's first thought as Constantinople slipped from view was that this was the first time he had ever sailed from a port that wasn't in chaos from an evacuation. But his next thought as he turned his face toward the west, toward America, was that he would do all he could to satisfy Kenneth O'Dell—right up to the time when he had found his Katya in America and convinced her to let him into her life and bed.

Then he sighed, reminding himself what the last four years had taught him—to take his happiness and pleasures as he could find them and not to take the future for granted. He was happy with Kenneth O'Dell. Katya could remain as a dream out there—somewhere. But he would not let dreams deny him the happiness that he and Kenneth could grasp if the dream was never to be his for the taking.

About the Author

DIRK HESSIAN

An artist and writer, Dirk has always been interested in history and legends, particularly those of the United States, the Mediterranean, and Asia. His works are historical, and sometimes border on fantasy. They are full of ordinary men struggling to survive and find love in difficult situations. And sometimes Dirk writes about men who are in touch with forces beyond those of mortal men, fighting for survival in more unusual ways.

Dirk's books often, but not always, contain male sex that is both forceful and rough, and at times dangerous, but is always within the context of stories of survival in more primitive and brutal times. He also writes about the power of love in turbulent times.

He can be found at the adults only gay male site www.BarbarianSpy.com, which he shares with Sabb and habu (sr71plt).

Our authors always like to receive feedback, and appreciate it when readers post reviews at Goodreads, Amazon, and other sites.

BarbarianSpy
FOR LITERARY HEAT

Not all books listed below may currently be on release.
* indicates the book is available in paperback and e-book.

BOOKS BY DIRK HESSIAN

Xtreme Erotica

The King's Men
Shores of Tripoli
Prophecy of Noto
Pretender's Fate

General Erotica/Romance

Fire Down the Valley*
Constantinople*
The Beautiful Way*
Blue and Gray
Colonel's Treasure
Beginning of Time
Labyrinth

BOOKS BY HABU

Gay Erotica

Memoir Faction

Flying High, Diving Deep*

Xtreme Erotica

Apyko: The Greek Pimp
Visits of the Schlange
Second Coming: Emile La Cour Unleashed
Vortex: Sacrificed by Curiosity*
Dark Angel Sounding *(in e-book & included in
Sounding:Ultimate Control Paperback)**
Sounding: Ultimate Control (*Print Only*)*
Sounding Five *(in e-book & included in
Sounding:Ultimate Control paperback)**

General Erotica

Romance

Snowy, Snowy Nights (Christmas Romance)

Four Coins
Lower Than the Heart
Brambleton
Gotta Keep Trying
Finding Amnad
Platres Conclave
Other Novels/Novellas
Cruising Gigolo
Prepared in Cape Verdi
Gilded Cage
House on Park
Anything for Ambition
Dance of the Ravishers
Hard Knocks U*
My Neighbor's Spa*
Man's Man: Tales of a High Priced Gay Hooker*
Trip Money
Clint Folsom Mysteries Compendium Volume 1*
Death to Blonds - Stolen Judgment (Clint Folsom Mystery)*
Clint Folsom Mysteries Compendium Volume 2*
The Indian Doctor
Sailorboy
Home to Fire Island
Choke Hold
Gay Erotica Anthologies
Spy Tales 001*
Spy Tales 002*
Doubled*
Doubled Again*
Tails in the Tropics*
Tails in the Med*
Tails in the West*
Rough Riders*
Grab Bag 1*
Grab Bag 2*
Grab Bag 3*
Grab Bag 4*

Grab Bag 5*
Beyond the Beaded Curtain*
Habu's Christmas Balls
The Sporting Life*
Fetish Galore!*
Literary Gay Erotica
Cairo Surrender*
The Handyman*
Homeward Bound
Journey to Mirage*
Menage Erotica
Cruising Gigolo
13 Ways for Halloween
Luther*
The Indian Prince
Literary GLBT Fiction
Summer of Denial
BOOKS BY SHABBU
Finding Jason
Dirty Pool
Operation Black Jade
Cigars!*
Angel in the Barn
Gayly Complicated*
Despoiling David
The Tree of Idleness*
I Met a Man
The Interview
Rough Road to Happiness
BOOKS BY SABB
Hiring in Hollywood
The Legend of Holleystone Grange
Surprise Encounters
She is He
Wrong Man
Loyal to his King
Barbarian Tales - Book One - Traveler's Tales*
Barbarian Tales - Book Two - Journeys Begin*

Barbarian Tales - Book Three - The Inheritance*
Barbarian Tales - Book Four - Road to Persepolis*